THE NIGHTRUNNERS

THE NIGHTRUNNERS

JOE R. LANSDALE

The Nightrunners

Introduction by
DEAN R. KOONTZ

TOR
HORROR

A TOM DOHERTY ASSOCIATES BOOK
NEW YORK

Although real towns and cities are named in this novel, mythical towns are also named, and the street names used in accordance with real towns are often the product of the author's imagination. No character in this novel is meant to represent anyone alive or dead, and any resemblance my imaginary characters might have to real characters is purely unintentional and coincidental.

THE NIGHTRUNNERS

Copyright © 1987 by Joe R. Lansdale
Introduction copyright © 1987 by NKUI, Inc.

All rights reserved.

Portions of this novel, in slightly different form, first appeared in the November/December 1984 issue of *Mississippi Arts and Letters* as "A Car Drives By" and in the Winter 1985/6 issue of *Hardboiled* as "Boys Will Be Boys." The short story "The Shaggy House," which appeared in the Winter 1986 issue of *The Horror Show*, and "God of the Razor," which appeared in issue number 5 of *Grue*, were inspired by scenes and concepts originated in this book.

Published by arrangement with Dark Harvest Inc.

A TOR Book
Published by Tom Doherty Associates, Inc.
49 West 24 Street
New York, NY 10010

ISBN: 0-812-52123-4   Can. ISBN: 0-812-52124-2

First Tor edition: March 1989

Printed in the United States of America

0 9 8 7 6 5 4 3 2 1

This book is dedicated to my wife, Karen. When times got hard she stuck by me. When pages wouldn't come she pulled them out of me. And when all looked lost she found what was missing, time after time after time.

I love you, babe, and thanks.

Acknowledgments

Acknowledgments are in order for Jeff Banks, Bob LaBorde, Bill Crider, Scott Cupp, Marylois Dunn, Commander W. T. March, Ardath Mayhar, Ted Olsen, Ray Puechner, Lee Schultz and Lew Shiner. They were kind enough, in one form or another, to invest their time and/or encouragement into me and this book. Thanks for the effort, folks. It is much appreciated and not forgotten.

And special thanks must be given to Keith Jordan Lansdale, my son. His imminent arrival helped me push the keys just a little bit faster back when this book was taking final shape.

Dark Harvest Press would like to express their gratitude to the following people. Thank you: Dawn Austin, Kathy Jo Camacho, Stan and Phyllis Mikol, Therese Anne Austin, Jennifer Kopp, Stan Gurnick, Ph.D., Luis Trevino and the people of Savon printing, Wayne Sommers, Bertha Curl, Kurt Scharrer, Raymond, Teresa and Mark Stadalsky, Cindy Cargine, Ken Morris, Gary Fronk, Robert Beighley, Sharon Krisch, Linda Solar, Penny Solar, Eileen Messner, John Zielinksi, and Ann Cameron Williams.

And Special Thanks to Joe R. Lansdale, Dean R. Koontz, and Gregory Manchess.

INTRODUCTION
by Dean R. Koontz

I am thankful for many things. I am thankful that gnarly oak fungus is not a human disease. I am thankful that the Department of Motor Vehicles will grant a driver's license without requiring that the applicant eat a live reptile. I am thankful that stairs lead up and down at the same time and that escalators do not. I am thankful that it is not a Western tradition to drink horse blood on Christmas Eve. I am thankful that socks are not made of barbed wire and that hailstones are seldom the size of apartment buildings. And I am thankful that Joe Lansdale decided to become a writer.

He swears that he once wanted to be a tater baron. For those who have no ear for Texas idiom, a tater baron is a farmer who makes a fortune raising and selling potatoes —an oil baron with roots. Joe had a piece of land, a good mule or two, a few bags of potato seeds (or whatever the devil they plant in order to grow the things), and plenty of determination. If he'd had a bit more luck in agriculture, we might know him today as the main supplier of spuds to McDonald's and Burger King. Misfortune smiled on him, however, and potatodom's loss is fiction's gain.

Joe was poor once, so his dreams of making a fast fortune in the potato industry are, though irrational, understandable. Those of us who have been poor are driven by a need for security that no one from a middle-class or wealthy family can ever understand.

Fortunately, although Joe was raised poor, his parents loved him, and they knew how to convey that love and warm him with it. He speaks of them with great affection; listening to him, one understands where he got the love of people that is apparent in the best of his fiction. "My father," Joe once told me, "was uneducated, and he could never earn much even though he worked hard. But what mattered was that he was a fine man, just the finest there could be, and if I never become a big-name writer, I'd count myself a success if I wound up being half as good a man as he was."

And he's sincere about that. You don't have to be around Joe a long time to realize that he means what he says and that, unlike many writers, he is not carrying a two-ton ego. Joe's one of those rare fellows who understands in his bones that selling a short story to *Twilight Zone* is not equivalent to the work done by leading cancer researchers and that selling a novel to Bantam, while desirable and exciting, ranks more than a notch or two below the achievements of Mother Teresa. You might be surprised, dear readers, to discover how many writers lack a reasonable perspective on their careers; they labor under the serious misapprehension that they are more important to the future of the world than all the rest of humankind combined. Joe is proud of his writing—and rightfully so; it's good—but he is incapable of forgetting that publication credits will never be as important as being a good husband, a good father, a good friend, and a good neighbor.

The funny thing is, truly first-rate work is seldom produced by those writers who campaign for awards, who have no doubt that their words will be in all the literature textbooks of the future, and who publicly compare themselves favorably with the old masters of the novel. On the other hand, the both-feet-firmly-on-the-ground Joes of this world frequently give us tales that are the essence of good writing. Maybe that's because the ain't-I-just-wonderful types are focused entirely on themselves, while the Joes are interested in other people and therefore are able to create characters that are real and convincing. And while the ain't-I-just-wonderful types are writing about Important Issues of which they know nothing, the Joes are writing about the mundane issues of daily existence in ways that illuminate them and move us, because the Joes understand that the mundane issues are also the eternal ones of life and death and hope and love and courage and meaning.

All of which is not to say that Joe Lansdale takes his work less seriously than he should. On the contrary, he cares deeply about his craft and his art, and that care is evident in his fiction.

I remember the night I picked up Joe Lansdale's *The Magic Wagon* and was at once enthralled by Billy Bob Daniels, Old Albert, Rot Toe the Wrestling Chimpanzee, the body in the box, and Buster Fogg. It was the strangest Western I'd ever read, full of creepy-crawly stuff as well as gunfighters, straddling genres with authority, and it dealt with the human condition in a profound yet unpretentious manner that any sensible writer would envy. In a fair world *The Magic Wagon* would have fallen into the hands of a publisher with the money and foresight to trumpet the Lansdale virtues to the world, and it might have become to the 1980s what *True Grit* was to its decade. Certainly, at the very least, if published as a mainstream novel with fanfare, *The Magic Wagon* would have made everyone aware that this man's ascension to the top ranks of Name Writers is not a matter of *if* but of *when*. This is not a fair world, however, and *The Magic Wagon* was published without fanfare by Doubleday as just another entry in its long-running line of Westerns. We should praise the editor who had the taste to recognize the value of that book—while reviling the system that condemned it to oblivion on its initial release.

Oblivion will not be the fate of future Lansdale novels. The only thing more certain than his eventual fame is tomorrow's sunrise. I suspect, however, that he is going to be one of those writers who takes a long time to build, who has to find his own readership with little assistance from his publishers. Many publishers don't really want to help writers build a following; instead they want to discover overnight successes who sell big from book one. The U.S. publishing industry stays busy spending fortunes on the latest illiterate Great Finds, who nearly always prove to have little talent and less staying power. While great riches and brief glory go to each year's newest sensations, real writers like Joe keep working steadily, getting better all the time; happily, the slow-track types frequently survive and ultimately prosper, while the overnight successes vanish into the great publishing swamp from which most of them should never have been dredged up in the first place. That's all right. Among the countless writers who have been slow-builders struggling against the industry's indifference, we can count John D. MacDonald, Elmore Leonard, Robert Heinlein, and Dick Francis, which is about the best company anyone could want.

The Nightrunners is early Lansdale. It is not as smooth or as polished or as strongly conceived as *The Magic Wagon* because this is a writer who grows book by book. Joe gets into some cold, dark places here, and perhaps he's nastier in this one than he really needed to be; restraint was something he was still learning when he wrote it. Is it entertaining? Oh, definitely. Will you get your money's worth? More than. This book has raw power. It is alive with the enthusiasm of a young writer going up against the blank page and getting one hell of a kick out of the challenge. It grabs you and carries you right along. Lansdale is so original that none of us can guess what new territory he will explore in his future books, but if we can't be sure where the wily varmint is going next, we can pick up *The Nightrunners* and at least find out where he's been. And where he's been is more interesting than anywhere a lot of other writers can ever hope to go.

I am thankful for many things. I am thankful that there are no known weather conditions in which dogs will spontaneously explode. I am thankful that Walt Disney gave us Mickey Mouse instead of Mickey Cockroach. I am thankful that the Hare Krishnas do not possess a nuclear arsenal. And I am thankful that Joe Lansdale decided to become a writer.

PROLOGUE:
A Black Shark Sails the Concrete Seas

October 29

"Well, yes! we are barbarians, and barbarians we wish to remain. It does us honor. It is we who will rejuvenate the world. The present world is near its end. Our only task is to sack it."

—Adolf Hitler

Midnight. Black as the heart of Satan.

They came rolling out of the darkness in a black '66 Chevy; eating up Highway 59 North like so much juicy, grey taffy. In the thickness of night, the car, all by its lonesome out there, seemed like a time machine from an evil future. Its lights were gold scalpels ripping apart the delicate womb of night, pushing forward through the viscera and allowing it to heal tightly behind it. The engine, smoothly tuned and souped-up heavy, moaned with sadistic pleasure.

Just two hours earlier, fifty miles outside of Houston, the Chevy had struck at a white Plymouth like a barracuda going for the belly of a tender white fish. The '73 Plymouth had been doing 60 miles an hour. It was in its own lane coming toward the Chevy, minding its own business, when the black demon crossed the stripe and its horn bellowed out through the murk. It wasn't a sound of warning, but a brazen peal of authority: *"Get out of the way, white fish, the road is mine!"*

The Plymouth, driven by a Houston insurance salesman named Jim Higgins, made a sudden jerk to the right and hit the shoulder, spewed up gravel, dirt, grass and a few careless crickets who should have been playing their fiddles somewhere else other than the edge of the highway.

Higgins had trouble with the vibrating steering

wheel, but he stayed with it. His teeth clacked together and his butt bounced in the seat, but he managed the Plymouth back on the road.

Higgins, who thought 60 miles an hour was adventurous, now floorboarded the Plymouth on up to 80. He let it ride there until the Chevy's taillights were pea-size, then nonexistent, but even then he only slowed to 70. He kept it there all the way to the edge of Houston where one of the city's finest pulled him over and gave him a ticket.

Higgins was almost glad to see the cop. It took the edge off the chill he was having. He nearly told the cop about the Chevy, but thought: "Naw, he'll just think I'm bullshitting him to get out of the ticket, and he might make it tough on me," so he was silent. He took the ticket and drove home.

Later that night he awoke screaming. Told his wife, Margret, that he had dreamed a black Chevy was bearing down on him, spurting fire and smoke from beneath its hood, and that inside the car, faces pressed against the windshield, were leering demons from hell.

At about the same time Jim Higgins was signing his speeding ticket, highway patrolman Vernice Trawler clocked the black Chevy at 90 miles an hour. Trawler's location was thirteen miles outside of Livingston, Texas. He blew out of his roadside hideaway with a blast of siren and rotating cherries, left half of his tires in smudge and smoke. Already the black Chevy was disappearing over the hill. The yellow line, blood-red in the glow of the Chevy's taillights, seemed to suck up behind the car.

Trawler gave his position over the radio, floorboarded the patrol car up to 70 . . . 80 . . . 90 . . . 95 . . . Now he could see the Chevy. It hardly seemed to touch ground.

"Sonofabitches," Trawler swore aloud. He was nearing the 100 mark now. When he caught up with this bastard it was going to be Ticket City.

Then suddenly, the Chevy seemed to toss out anchor. It broke down against the night, slacked to 70 . . . 60 . . . 50 . . . 40 in rabbitlike hops.

"Damn fine car," Trawler admitted aloud.

The Chevy pulled over to the shoulder, spewed up gravel and stopped.

Trawler pulled up behind it, wished suddenly that his partner wasn't out with the flu.

(Now why should I think that? Trawler considered. Why should that occur to me?)

Trawler's flashing red light threw a strobe show across the Chevy's back glass, showed him three heads in the back seat and two in the front.

The driver's door opened. A teenager with clean-cut features, shaggy blond hair and a too-white face stepped out of the car. He was wearing jeans, a jeans jacket and a grey sweatshirt underneath. He had on blue tennis shoes—*tenny runners,* Trawler's son called them.

Trawler sighed. Working by himself was uncomfortable, even if the worst he'd ever encountered were drunks and head-on collisions. This was just a kid—just a couple years older than his own. A carload of kids, out for a joyride in a souped-up car.

Nonetheless, Trawler loosened his gun in his holster, picked up his ticket book and got out, wary, but not really expecting trouble.

The blond kid was smiling. When Trawler was halfway to him, the kid said, "Guess I'm in for it, huh?"

"Didn't you see the lights?" Trawler asked. "Hear the sirens?"

"No sir."

"You don't use your rearview mirror?"

The kid shrugged.

Trawler flashed his flashlight into the Chevy. In the front seat sat a scrawny kid with brown, greasy hair down in his eyes. The kid looked back at Trawler, a slight smile on his face.

Drunk, maybe, Trawler thought.

Trawler moved the flash to the back seat where he could see a dark-haired girl of about seventeen sitting between the two boys. She was attractive, looked Mexican. The boy on her left was stocky and square-jawed with hardly any expression. The other was basketball-player tall with cadaverous features molded out of pimply, puttylike flesh and topped with a generous amount of carrot-colored hair.

Trawler barely heard when the boy answered his question.

"What was that?"

"The rearview mirror, *sir*. I didn't see you in it. I mean, I wasn't looking at first, *sir*."

Trawler had preferred the shrug. Now that the boy had decided to answer the question, the *sir* he was using had acquired a grating quality. It got on Trawler's nerves.

"Let me see your license, son."

"Yes, *sir*."

Why is this kid grinning like an idiot? Trawler wondered. Drinking?

The boy took his wallet from his back pocket, folded it open, fished out his license and reached it to Trawler with two fingers.

Just as Trawler was about to take it, the kid fumbled and the license fell to the ground.

"Pick that up, please," Trawler said.

The boy bent down, and as he did, Trawler heard the front passenger door open and saw the greasy-haired kid rise out of the car and twist across the roof of the Chevy with something in his hands—a sawed-off 12-gauge shotgun he had pulled from beneath the seat.

Even so, Trawler knew he had the kid dead to rights, for as soon as he heard the door squeak, his hand reached for his gun, and Trawler knew that he was fast, fast, fast . . .

What he didn't expect was the blond kid to come up from the ground with an uppercut to the groin and throw off his timing by a split second. A split second that made all the difference in the world. It was the kid's edge on Trawler's draw.

The shotgun had no pattern. It was loaded with slugs; straight-flying projectiles with incredible velocity. The shotgun fell into place against the roof of the Chevy and the sound of its blast filled up the night.

Trawler never heard it.

Just before his brain exploded, Trawler's last electric-fast thought was of a million black and grey fragments flying to him from all directions, like the vengeful flies of Beelzebub about to light.

PART ONE:
A Ripple of Fin

October 29–31

Evil communications corrupt good
manners.
> —Corinthians 15:33

And it came to pass . . . that Pharaoh
dreamed. And . . . his spirit was
troubled; and he sent and called for
all the magicians of Egypt, and all
the wise men thereof: and the
Pharaoh told them his dream. . . .
> —Genesis 41:1–8

pre·cog·ni·tion n. Knowledge of
something in advance of its
occurrence.
> —The American Heritage Dictionary

Deep into that darkness peering,
long
I stood there, wondering,
fearing . . .
> —Edgar Allan Poe, "The Raven"

ONE

Montgomery Jones looked at his watch. One A.M.
They were nearly to their destination and already
Becky was having the dreams again.

Well, he hadn't expected a mere change of
scenery to correct that, but right here, near the end
of their trip, at the true beginning of their vacation
—if that was the proper word—he took it as a bad
omen.

Becky slept fitfully in the back seat, tossing and
turning, making noises in her throat that reminded
him of an old dog his dad had owned. "Chasing
rabbits in his sleep, Monty," his dad used to say as
the sleeping dog kicked and whined.

Montgomery knew Becky wasn't chasing rabbits,
however. Something was chasing her; the dark side
of a memory.

He hoped this trip would help dilute those
memories. He knew that it would not eliminate
them. Like smallpox scars they would remain, but
perhaps they could be doctored into a benign state
of existence.

He hoped.

Montgomery turned on the windshield wipers as
rivulets of rain gathered on the glass. Less than five
minutes ago the sky had been black and crisp and
full of shimmering, ice-blue stars. But that was East
Texas weather for you. As the old tired joke went,
"If you don't like the weather here, wait a minute."

To the best of his memory, he had the directions right, and this was the road coming up. He turned the VW Rabbit off the blacktop and onto a narrow path of red clay that ambled its way into the forest of crowding pines.

"You've got plenty of privacy there," Dean had said. "No one to bother you. Not a house within three miles. Swell place. Relaxing. Quiet. Becky'll love it, and you will too. Do you good. Pines all around, a lake out back, plenty of fresh air. Swell place."

That phrase of Dean's hung in Montgomery's memory like barbed wire. *Swell place.*

The trip had gone badly from the first. One fuckup after another. He hadn't taken it too seriously at first, but now, coupled with Becky's dreams, it all seemed earthshaking.

Then again, one A.M. had a way of making things seem terribly traumatic.

"Take her away for a while," the psychiatrist had said. "Let her have a change of scenery. Being in the apartment where it happened isn't a good idea. Make arrangements to move. And in the meantime, get away. She's trying to be strong about it, but the passing months haven't helped that much. It's eating her up inside. Take her on a vacation for a week or so and find plenty to do. You might be surprised at how much of a change it will make."

So he had heeded the psychiatrist's advice. They left Galveston and stopped off in Houston to eat at a rather famous and highly recommended restaurant, and what happens but Becky gets sick. Something she ate. And the damn food hadn't been that good either. Thirty-five dollars for something that tasted like what the dog threw up, and an upset stomach for Becky to boot.

Next stop had been the Alabama-Coushatta Indian reservation. But this year it had rained like hell and the water had risen out of the Big Thicket and swamped both train ride and reservation. Snakes were everywhere, and all the tours were closed down. Only the Trading Post was open, and everything sold there was twentieth-century bright and made in the Orient. About the only thing the Indians had to do with the "crafts" was unloading them from a truck.

(Get your gen-U-ine im-I-tation Alabama-Coushatta In-dee-an trinkets rightchere, folks. Hurry and getem, won't be another boat from Japan for a month.)

The government and the reservation's administrators had turned the place into a clown act.

Take the reservation trip, pile the shitty restaurant on top of that, add Becky getting sick, and now the goddamn dreams, and what you had was October 29 whipped into one, thick, depressing shit pie.

Red clay widened a bit, rolled into a circle drive. A long, low, ranch-style cabin projected out of the pines. The lake lay not far behind it.

Cabin, hell. It looked like the Ritz to Montgomery, logs or not. It was easily three to four times the size of their apartment.

Montgomery wheeled the Rabbit around the drive and stopped with the lights resting on the cabin. He looked back at Becky, reached out and touched her gently on the hip. She came quick-awake with the same wild-eyed stare that had been assaulting him every morning for the past month. It made him think of an animal that had been caged and antagonized by man.

He smiled with effort. "What do you think?"

Cataracts of dreadful memory fell from her eyes. Her face softened. She leaned forward, rested her arms on the front seat and looked at the house. "Big," she said.

Montgomery tried not to let his feelings show, but he was devastated. Becky's face disturbed him, as it had for some time now. Something alien had moved in behind the flesh. She looked more like thirty-five than twenty-five. Her hair, normally well brushed and luster brown, hung to her sagging shoulders like a dead hope. Her once-sharp features seemed curbed by swollen flesh. But the eyes were the worst. There were times when they actually frightened him.

Becky put her hands in her lap, left hand folded over the right. A psychiatrist would say Becky was holding her hands over her privates like that because of the rape. And goddamnit, they would be right.

"Becky?"

"Huh . . . Sorry, my mind was elsewhere."

On your back with a rapist astride, perhaps. A cold, sharp knife at your throat? Was that where it was?

God, poor baby.

He reached over the seat and took her hand. There was a slight, reflexive pull on her part, and her fingers felt like frozen metal pipes to his touch. He let go of her and got out of the car.

She opened her door and he said, "Wait a minute. I'll unlock it."

He walked to the cabin and used the key Dean had given him. Inside it was musty and warm. Quite a contrast from the cool rain on his neck.

Feeling along the wall, he found the light switch, flicked it on.

Redwood walls and soft, rust-colored carpets were revealed. There was very little furniture, but what was there was simple and attractive: a couch, two stuffed chairs, a coffee table, and to his right, a bar and pantries. A few stools. Beyond that, through a doorless, wide opening, was a kitchen. Porcelain winked from the darkness there.

He walked into the kitchen and turned on the light. The kitchen was large. About half the size of their apartment, it seemed.

He walked back through the living room and looked in the bathroom. Very nice. Bright blue tile with matching walls and shower curtain.

The bedroom was cozy and well decorated too. The second bathroom was still in the process of construction. Hammers, nails and all manner of tools were strewn about. Sheets of paneling leaned against the wall and there were two-by-fours on the floor. "You'll just have to shut the door and not look in there," Eva had said. "Dean and I just work on the place summers, so it lacks some being finished."

Montgomery went back to the door and waved Becky inside.

Sure, he thought. Come on in. Your big protector has scoped it out.

Well, where were you when your wife was being raped, big protector?

Attending a nice, comfortable sociology conference in Houston, that's where. Subject: The Alienation of the Juvenile.

Nice and ironic that. So ironic he wanted to cry. Again.

And what would you have done had the cabin been occupied by a burglar, even a belligerent drunk, big protector?

Crap your pants, maybe?

Water your socks with urine?

Would that be a good guess?

Until recently, the totally nonviolent philosophy

he had lived by had seemed logical. Very logical. Violence solves nothing.

"No man ever did a designed injury to another without doing a greater to himself." That's what Henry Home had said. He had memorized the words in college, and made them his motto. His standard. The banner he carried before him.

Ah, but had Henry Home's wife been raped? Had he experienced the boiling in his blood that such an act causes? Had he felt the festering of his soul? Had he dreamed of taking such molesters in his hands—suddenly made of steel, spiked all over and spring-loaded—and ripping, squeezing them apart like wet newspaper?

He had. Many times.

Before the rape, things had been simpler. During the Vietnam War he had been so certain; had known exactly where he stood and why.

"*You wish to sign as a Conscientious Objector?*"

"*Yes, Sergeant, I do.*"

"*You are opposed to violence of any kind?*"

"*I am.*"

"*You are not merely opposed to the Vietnam War, but to violence itself?*"

"*I said as much.*"

"*You would not raise your hand to protect your home?*"

"*I could not kill another human being.*"

"*Even to save your own life?*"

"*No. I could not kill.*"

And the sergeant had looked at him long and hard, pitying. And he had felt so superior to that sergeant. He had thought: What a stupid, military mind. He can't stand a rational, thinking human being. All he can think is Kill! Kill! Kill! He thinks I'm a coward instead of a moralist.

Well, old buddy, are you a coward?

Was the sergeant right? Have you been fooling yourself all these years?

Is the truth more like the fifth grade when Billy Sylvester beat you to a nubbin and kicked you in the balls and made you like it?

Is it more like that?

Like when you paid Billy half your lunch money so he wouldn't beat the cowardly crap out of you every day?

More like that?

Or like when Billy forced you to watch while he fed your little brother, Jack, a dog turd?

Remember Billy saying (smiling while he did, holding the dog turd with an old candy wrapper, holding your brother down with his knee), "Smile while he eats it, pussy."

Remember that?

Hey, hey, hey. Remember smiling?

And remember your brother, Jack, dogshit masked on his teeth, kicking and struggling, being more of a man than you ever were?

Remember Billy going away laughing? Can you still hear the echo of that laughter rocking around inside your head?

Okay. You were right about the Vietnam War, Mr. Smart Guy. Time has proved you out on that one. But was part of your reason for not going more barnyard than political or intellectual? Was there really a plump chicken heart beating against your educated breast?

"Not bad," Becky said.

Montgomery swam out of it. "Yeah . . . nice."

Becky set her bag inside the door and looked around, her hands once again folded in front of her, protectively.

Would you stop that, Montgomery thought, but said, "Come on in and take a look."

He walked over and put his arm around her shoulders.

She wilted.

He removed the arm slowly. No way he could even force a smile now.

"It's not you, Monty . . . Really . . . it's not . . . You know that."

"Yeah."

"I love you . . . believe me . . . I try every day. It's just hard right now. I'll be better . . . it just takes time."

"Sure," Montgomery said, wondering if things could ever be as they had been before. It all seemed rather perfect then.

Becky smiled. There was the faintest impression of her old self there, but it was fleeting. "Really, Monty. I'm sorry."

He nodded. "It's okay. I'll get the rest of the stuff out of the car."

The rain felt good against his flushed face. He got the bags from the Rabbit, started back to the cabin.

Becky stood just inside the doorway, looking in. But Montgomery knew she wasn't seeing the living room. She was tuned inward, examining an endless replay of her rape in Technicolor and stereophonic sound.

He stepped around her and into the room.

Becky turned and smiled at him. An empty smile.

He smiled back, and still holding the bags, he hooked the door with his foot and kicked it closed.

It slammed much harder than he expected.

TWO

The dreams had started immediately after the rape.

Of course, it was normal that horrible dreams should follow such an experience, but somehow, Becky felt they were something other than dreams.

Knew they were.

They didn't come only in sleep. They weren't selective. Asleep. Wide awake. Didn't matter. They came. Flashing before her internal vision like moving pictures. It could happen anytime without notice. Washing dishes. Taking a bath. Reading. Even watching television.

The damn things had destroyed her already confused life.

At first she had actually considered continuing her teaching, but found she couldn't. She kept thinking that some of the students in her class—perhaps friends of Clyde Edson, her rapist—were watching her, wondering how it had been for old Clyde and if she liked it. The thought of it made her want to scream, "I hated it!"

Once she had done just that. Sat upright in bed and screamed those words.

Terrified poor Monty. But most things seemed to. He didn't like to plug in electrical appliances, or take a bath in water over a foot deep. He was afraid to light fires. He didn't like heights. He didn't like crowds, made him nervous.

Skitty Monty, that was him.

Right now he was in the kitchen boiling water for instant coffee, probably terrified that the water would leap out of the pan at him.

God, thought Becky, I certainly come down hard on him. Monty wasn't the one who raped me (actually, there had been several, but she could only remember Clyde's face and the others seemed more like extensions of him); wasn't the one who held a knife to my throat while he grunted out his passion, slobbering on my shoulder and face as he did.

Perhaps, she thought (as she often did), I should have forced Clyde to use the knife. At least there wouldn't be the dreams.

Dreams? Well, that wasn't exactly right. There had been dreams all right, but these others . . . what were they?

Visions?

That was the only word that struck her right.

She remembered the first visions as clearly as if they had occurred moments ago.

It was less than a week after the rape. Monty had gone to bed early that night, and she, in need of some sort of brain drain, stayed up to watch Johnny Carson and then the flickering snow of a dead television set.

And the images came to her. Clearer than Carson and Rickles had been an hour earlier.

She not only saw, but she experienced the moment of Clyde's death; felt the emotional intensity of it, as if she were living inside his head.

She could still see/feel the knotted shirt strips about his neck. Feel his sudden regret as he kicked away from the wall and let go of the window bars, allowed himself to dangle like a rope over an abyss, flapping back from time to time to slap the wall.

His face went blue. His boiled-egg eyes (reminiscent of when he had exploded his orgasm inside her) seemed about to leap from his head. The shirt strips were slicing into his throat, blood was welling around them—

—and she came to on the floor of the living room, coated in sweat, her nightgown sticking to her as if glued.

Just a dream, she thought. Wonderful in its own vengeful way, but still, just a dream.

But the next morning the images came again while she was showering. Fine spray from the shower head turned to long, light-colored strands that wove into a noose, and suddenly Clyde hung from it, blue-tongued, puppetlike, the cloth biting into his neck, forming first a red welt, then a blue-bruise collar that turned to black.

The image maintained for a moment, weakened, faded away.

Becky sagged to her knees.

Water beat down on her in a warm, pleasing rhythm.

God, but it had felt good. Her best daydream ever. Clyde getting his. Wish fulfillment to the one-hundreth power.

Or so she thought.

A moment later, while she was toweling off, the phone rang. She threw on a bathrobe and made for it. Monty, who was enjoying his Saturday morning with a book, came up behind her, waiting to see who the caller might be. He looked the question at her and she formed the silent word "Philson."

Both Sergeant Philson and his wife had been very kind throughout the ordeal, and Becky thanked the fates that he was the one assigned to her case. He was understanding; didn't look at her as if she had given the kids the come-on; didn't treat her like a flophouse whore. He was the kind that gave cops a good name.

It was strange news he delivered, and his voice seemed undecided on how to tell it.

"The Edson boy," he finally said. "He hung himself in his cell."

Becky felt not a drop of grief. She stood there with the phone to her face, and after a moment, she realized Philson was still talking.

She gave the phone to Monty, leaned against the wall in a daze, listened as he spoke to Philson; spoke words to match his liberal position; words about how bad it was a boy so young had wasted his life. Too bad. He was real sorry. Perhaps in time he might have rehabilitated, mumble, mumble, mumble.

Hypocrite. She knew he hadn't meant a word of it. It went with his cowardice, his inability to go against his trained sociological thinking, his inability to toss out his liberal crutch.

To Monty's way of thinking no one had to be accountable for their actions. There was always the environment and parents and poor potty training to blame. The individual was never responsible. Each and every one of us was nothing more than a rudderless boat adrift on a sea of fate, constantly in search of a snug harbor and its protection against the ragings of environmental storms.

Or so went the philosophy of Montgomery Jones.

After he hung up the phone, she told him about the visions, and he had smiled, talked about strains and wishful thinking.

It made her mad, but at the time she thought he might be right. But as the days passed, she recalled the vision, and became certain that it was real; knew for a fact that she had been in tune with Clyde the moment he had taken the sweet plunge. It was as if the rape had inextricably linked her with him, formed a sort of psychic umbilical cord that had been severed with his dying.

How she would have loved to have been there— and in a way she had had the next best thing, a psychic ringside seat—when he stepped into space. She could have asked him how he liked it, how it felt. The same questions he had asked her during the rape.

Monty interrupted her thoughts, came in with two cups of coffee, that stupid smile on his face. The same stupid smile he wore when she first told him of the dream; the patronizing, good-husband smile he tacked on while he soothed her and prepared the way for the psychiatrist.

And the idiot psychiatrist had worn the same stupid smile. And he had a mile of jargon: "Mrs. Jones, there is no evidence for the existence of clairvoyant dreams. These dreams are the result of a drastic emotional and psychological trauma. Nothing more. It only seemed that you dreamed of the boy's death in the exact manner it happened.

"It gave you a sense of revenge, and you have convinced yourself it was a vision, when in fact, your mind tricked you. Such a thing is not uncommon.

"In time, these dreams, these visions as you call them, will go away. Forget this psychic mumbo jumbo. There's a very logical explanation for this contained within the electrical impulses of your brain. Now go home. Try and forget. Time will ease the pain, and the dreams will go away."

But they had not. And each mention of them to

Monty earned her a sympathetic nod, and that goddamn smile.

She sipped her coffee, looked over the cup at Monty.

He smiled the silly smile.

The rain danced more briskly on the cabin roof.

THREE

Later, after a vain attempt to entertain themselves with small talk, Monty and Becky gave it up and went to bed.

The rain grew heavier, and the rhythmic beat of it on the roof lulled them to sleep.

And less than fifty miles away, the '66 Chevy rolled along, drawing itself up the concrete line of the highway like a yo-yo engulfing a string.

FOUR

In the dark, when hit from time to time by the light of flashing skies, Malachi Roberts' skin looked purple.

He lay in bed with the sheets pulled halfway down across his thick chest, watched the lightning come and go outside his window. Watched the rain fall. Listened to the low growl of gentle thunder; an occasional Chinese gong crash that shook the house.

Malachi sighed. He could not sleep, and it was not because of what was happening outside his window. Not the rain, the lightning, not even the thunder. He was lonesome somehow. The pit of his stomach felt as empty as the end of the world and his heart was wet slush in his chest.

Careful, so as not to awaken his wife, he slipped his worn body from beneath the sheets and sat on the edge of the bed, looked out the window and wished for clear skies and plenty of daylight.

Lightning flashed.

His black skin jumped purple. Jumped back black again.

Holding up his hand, he spread his fingers and waited for the sky to explode once more.

It did.

Black fingers went purple. Purple went black.

He grinned to himself. He felt like a kid. When he was a boy he used to do that; watch the lightning between his fingers, see the color the quick-flash made his skin.

For a moment, loneliness left him, but like a bounding flea it leapt right back.

Rising slowly, wearing nothing but his undershorts, he padded softly into the kitchen.

Maybe he was hungry.

Rain cascaded down one corner of the kitchen, gathered whispering into a big black pot.

Damn, Malachi thought. Every time it rained, same thing. He'd been telling himself he was going to fix that leak for over a year now. But when it was dry, he didn't think of it. It was amazing Dorothy didn't complain more.

Malachi knew that he was not a lazy man, but after a day of turning bolts and dipping his hands in grease and oil and gasoline and crawling over the insides of cars, he just didn't want to do anything with his hands.

What he wanted to do was sit on his front porch, smoke his pipe and watch the world go by on the highway. Or watch his snowy television set, or take his woman to bed.

But that damned leak.

Angry at himself, he went to the refrigerator, got a half gallon of milk out, drank right from the carton.

No. That wasn't what he wanted.

He sat down at the kitchen table, the carton of milk in front of him.

From where he sat, he could see out the window above the sink, could watch the lightning sew a crazy stitch across the sky. It was really getting fierce out there, and it didn't show any signs of slacking off.

He glanced at the kettle. It was almost full. He'd have to empty it now if he didn't want it running over before morning.

Taking another draught of the milk, he returned it to the refrigerator, crept back to the bedroom, pulled on his pants and slipped on his shoes without bothering with socks.

After looking at the sleeping form of his wife, and smiling, he tiptoed back to the kitchen, quietly rummaged a pan from beneath the cabinet.

Being as careful as possible, he slid the kettle aside and replaced it with the pan.

For a moment, water struck the pan with a sound like dried peas falling.

Malachi glanced apprehensively toward the bedroom.

Usually, the slightest noise would awaken Dorothy, but tonight she slept like a rock. Unusual for her.

He was glad of that, her health being what it was. Her blood pressure had been giving her a particularly hard time of late. She needed all the rest she could get.

After a moment of waiting, of listening for bedsprings or padding feet—for he fully expected Dorothy to appear in the bedroom doorway with hands on hips and a wry smile on her face—he took the heavy black kettle and began duck walking it toward the front porch.

He set it down temporarily to prop the door and screen open, then managed it onto the porch, tilted the water over the side. It made a loud noise as it hit the bare and muddy flower bed below.

He glanced back inside the house.

So far so good.

Leaving the kettle on the porch, he went inside and got his pipe and tobacco off the drainboard. He packed it, lit it, went back outside for a smoke. This time he closed the door behind him.

He looked out at his yard. Just one big mud pie. Beyond it, the surface of Highway 59 appeared to boil. Above him, the tin roof rattled and trembled beneath the buckshot rain.

Then he saw the light. Way out on the highway, coming from the south; car lights made fuzzy by the rain.

He thought whoever was driving that crate was going much too fast; cruising like they had bone-dry highways and lots of light.

"Gonna end up in a goddamn ditch," he said around the stem of his pipe.

And now the car was splashing by with a hungry roar—

—and Malachi felt cold; more so than any rain should make him, even a late October rain. The wet slush in his chest that had been serving as a heart turned to a fist of hard ice.

He shivered.

For a moment it was as if nothing else lived in the universe but him.

Lightning flashed, lit the night bright as day. Malachi could see the car clearly—a black '66 Chevy turning off 59 onto the Old Minnanette Highway, which was hardly a highway at all anymore.

Then it was night again and there were only the taillights winking away in the cold, dark sockets of night and the growl of the engine receding in the distance.

Suddenly the driver hit down on his horn.

Once.

Twice.

Three times.

Sharp, harsh punctures in the messy, wet night.

Then silence.

Malachi shivered again. Thought: It's as if Old Man Death himself just drove by with his window cranked down and his breath leaking out; the rotten, chilling breath of the sick and the dying.

After a moment the sensation passed. Malachi thumped the contents of his pipe out and hauled the kettle inside, put it in its place and put the pan away.

Then, removing his shoes, pinching them between thumb and forefinger, he stole silently back to the bedroom, pushed the shoes beneath the bed and removed his pants. He eased softly under the bedclothes and for a moment lay still on his back, looking at the ceiling.

Dorothy did not awake.

He had it made now.

Gently, he rolled on his side and put his arm around her—and felt the marble-cool flesh of the recently dead.

FIVE

October 30, 1:30 A.M.

The black car pulled off the Old Minnanette Highway and rolled down a wet, clay road. It found harbor in front of a barbed-wire cattle gate. Sat there while the sky went about its wet tantrum.

After a moment, a back door opened. A girl got out, moved across the road and into the woods behind the car. She found a place thick with overhead branches and surrounding foliage, dropped her pants, squatted to pee.

She could see the car from where she squatted, and even in the darkness, she could see the white face of the driver. It was pressed up against the door glass, looking out at the night. It didn't look quite human, a white, pasty thing with gun-barrel eyes; eyes loaded with hate and fury.

She shivered.

"Blessed Mother," she mumbled to herself, "how did I get into this?"

All she wanted was a wedding. The sort with a veil, a long bridal train dragging behind her. Nothing more. Except Jimmy dressed in a suit instead of greasy jeans and jacket for a change.

That was hardly what she had gotten.

But then, not getting what she wanted or expected had become a way of life for her.

It had always been that way.

Each day was just one bigger shit-brick than the last.

Her first memories of her father were of him speaking Spanish drunkenly, fondling her between the legs—until her mother caught him one night, and that was the last she saw of him. Here today. Gone tomorrow. No big loss.

The thing she remembered best after that was her mother constantly making her strip and lie on the bed so she could explore with cold hands—always cold hands—the inside of her snatch. Make sure she was still a virgin. This was an obsession

with her mother, making sure her daughter was
unsoiled.

She went out on a date, her mother would be
waiting. Then she'd get the strip, cold fingers in
the snatch routine.

If her mother suspicioned she had been near
boys, it was the strip, cold fingers in the snatch
routine.

Look at a boy's picture too long in a magazine, it
was the strip, cold fingers in the snatch routine.
What was she expecting to find in there? The
refuse of wood-pulp jism? Was the guy in the
magazine going to come out of the picture and stick
a paper dick in her? What was the deal?

The routine got to be daily.

She began to think maybe her mother just liked
smelling her fingers afterward. That and looking at
her religious crap were her only pastimes. Had the
shit all over the house. A living room full of tiny
Blessed Mother shrines and crosses. And in the
kitchen, over the sink, so she could watch it while
she did the dishes, there was a five-dollar plastic
Jesus with batteries and a lightbulb inside. Touch
the switch—cleverly located in the statue's side
wound—and J.C.'s eyes glowed like a cat in the
dark.

And there was that stupid *700 Club* blaring all
the time. Lots of preachers in expensive suits with
hair sprayed down hard enough to look like concrete curbing.

It was enough to drive a madman sane.

Some life.

Then she met Jimmy. Ugly, pimple-faced Jimmy.

But he was nice and interested in marrying her,
could take her away from the shrines and the *700
Club*.

She met him one day after school. He was sitting on the hood of an old battered white Ford. When she walked by he yelled, "Hey," and she stopped.

He climbed down off the hood of the car, went over to her.

"Hey, I'm Jimmy. What's your name?"

"Why do you need to know, taking a survey?"

"'Cause I wanta."

"Why?"

"I like the way you look."

"No kidding, so do a lot of other guys."

"Yeah, I bet."

"Really?"

"Sure. You say so, I believe it. Besides, look at you."

"That some kind of crack?"

"Naw, no way. I mean, look at you. You look good. Lots of guys would like the way you look, just like me. I mean, you could probably have any guy you want."

"Yeah, yeah, maybe I could."

"You could."

"Yeah, okay, I could."

"Now, will you tell me your name?"

"I guess . . . Angela."

"Nice name."

"Yeah, well, Jimmy isn't so hot. I had a hamster named Jimmy. My mother killed it with a broom."

"So it's not a good name. Do I look like a hamster to you?"

"A little."

He smiled. "Carry your books, Angela?"

"I guess."

He put her books under his arm and started walking toward the Ford. "I'll give you a lift. Where you going?"

She thought a moment. "Nowhere," she said, and meant it.

At first he was something to fill the hours, someone to spend time with after school. And each day, after she left him, and after her mother made with the exploration through the country of her privates, she would find herself looking forward to the night, to when he came to her window. He'd sneak up the back alley and scratch on the screen and they'd talk, sometimes until way into the morning. Talk was all they did, nothing more. She never even unlatched the screen.

Jimmy never tried any funny business with her, just told her he loved her and wanted to marry her.

It was an idea, she told him, but he didn't have a job. What were they going to live on?

He admitted it was a problem.

Shortly thereafter, he dropped out of school and got a janitor job at the Galveston courthouse. Didn't pay much, but it was something.

Each week he brought her the bulk of his earnings, and now she was unlocking the screen, taking the money, holding his hand, and leaning forward to take his lips.

Things were looking good for Angela baby, and that should have been a clue.

Because suddenly, it was shit-brick time again.

Yep, she could count on it. Soon as she started having a pretty good time and things started looking up, the shit-bricks would fall.

Angela's feeling good. Look out! Here comes the shit-bricks.

Angela's luck looks like it's going to change, and watch it! Because here comes a whole wall of tumbling shit-bricks, right down on top of her little Puerto Rican head.

This time was no exception.

The first shit-brick to fall was not the last, not by any means, but it was certainly a doozy. Hit right smack on the head of her dream.

Jimmy got buddies, and suddenly he was a tough guy. Started seeing her less, and when he did come around he'd say: "I'm not so sure about this marriage stuff. How do I know you're going to be a good piece of ass? I mean, I haven't seen any action."

She let that go for a while, then one night, while he was singing the same song, one hundreth verse, she said: "Whatever happened to my nice Jimmy?"

That seemed to get him a bit, but he said, "Part of my problem. Too much Mr. Nice Guy. What's it got me?"

"After we're married you can have me."

"After we're married, after we're married, that's all I ever hear about. You got stock in marriage licenses? I'm not so sure I want to get married anymore. I mean, I might be getting a pig in a poke, you know what I mean? Or maybe a pig that won't poke, know what I mean?"

"What's with you? . . . You're different."

"I'm learning some things about women."

"From your friends?"

"Yeah, they've taught me some stuff. Sure. Real cool guys."

"Things like how to treat women?"

"Things like that."

"You love me, don't you, Jimmy?"

"Yeah, I guess. . . . I'm just not sure I want to get married until I've sampled the water, you know what I mean? Get in there and get my feet wet."

"Why buy the cow when you can get the milk for free?"

"What's that?"

"Think about it."

"Don't try and turn the tables on me, Angela."

"I'm not trying, you asshole, I'm doing. I don't care much for the new Jimmy. You can take these new friends of yours and shove them up your ass."

"Hey, you're getting loud. Your mother will hear."

"What do you care? I'm giving you your money back."

"Hey, why's that? We're getting married."

"Who's getting married? You haven't gotten to sample the water." She started away from the window.

"Say, Angela, I'm sorry, baby. Really."

"Mean it?" she said, turning back to him.

"Yeah . . . Yeah, I mean it."

"You sure?"

"I said so."

"Just being the tough guy for no good reason?" Silence.

"Come on, say it, Jimmy."

Nothing.

"I'll get your money."

"Okay, okay . . ." Softly: "Just being a tough guy. No good reason."

"Where I can hear you."

"I said it, that's enough."

"Want me to get you money?"

"Yeah, get the fucking money. I've had it."

"Fine." She started across the room.

He called through the window, just above a whisper. "Sorry."

She turned. "Did some wind blow through here or something, or did I hear you talking?"

"Sorry," he said.

"How sorry are you, Jimmy?"

"For Christsakes, what do you want from me?"

"I want the old Jimmy back, the one without the tough mouth and the tough-guy friends. The one that cries at movies when they're sad."

"Goddamnit, I don't."

She smiled. "I've seen you. It's okay."

A moment of silence. Then: "I'm sorry. Real sorry. These guys, they say I let you push me around too much. That I see you too much. They say I'm pussy-whipped."

"How's that? You don't get any."

"Well, they don't know that."

"So you been telling them how it is with hot little Angela?"

"Not exactly."

"But you suggest?"

"Sort of . . . I mean it isn't manly for me not to . . . You know?"

She crossed the room, rested her elbows on the windowsill. He moved his hands up, clutched her elbows gently. Softly, shyly, he said: "Sorry."

"Yes, you are."

"Don't deny it. It's just that . . . well, I want to run with these guys. They're neat . . . and they got this house. I thought when we got married we could move there. Wouldn't cost us much. Later . . . well, later we could get us an apartment."

"Who are these guys?"

"Real cool heads."

"Who are they?"

"Just some guys I met around the pool hall. They got this big house and some girls live there with them sometimes."

"Change girls like socks, huh?"

"Guess. I don't know. Don't care."

"Jimmy?"

"Yeah?"

"You're acting like an asshole. Your friends sound like assholes. All they're good for is trouble, I know it."

"You don't know them."

"I don't need to. I can smell them on you, and I don't like the stink."

"I'm not acting like an asshole. And they're not assholes neither."

"Take my word for it, you, them, assholes. Big ones."

Jimmy sighed. "You're the hardest girl I ever did know."

"Assholes."

"All right, assholes. I'm an asshole and they're assholes. Happy?"

"Completely."

"Good. Real good."

"Jimmy, we don't want to live in any crummy house with this bunch of assholes that are making you an asshole, now do we?"

Jimmy didn't quite grit his teeth. "I guess not."

"Can you climb through this window?"

Silence. He looked at her strangely.

"Are you deaf? Can you climb through this window? Answer me that, can an asshole like yourself climb through this window?"

"I can do that."

"You want to climb through?"

"You say so, yeah."

She stood up, pulled her shirt over her head. Unfastened her bra. Her breasts small, dark and firm bounced free.

Jimmy got through that window in record time. She had her pants off now, her underwear.

Then they were in bed and he was pounding her
for all he was worth, and she was getting about as
much pleasure out of it as the bag down at the gym
that the prizefighters train on, when suddenly the
bedroom door opened and the light came on and
her mother shrieked, grabbed the old teddy bear
off Angela's dresser and began pounding Jimmy
briskly about the head and ears.

Jimmy rolled off the bed, scooped up his clothes
and like a seal leaping off a rock, dove through the
window and out into the night.

Still clutching the stuffed bear, Angela's mother
turned on her, breathing like an asthmatic hippo.

"Know what, Momma?" Angela said. "You won't
have to check this time. Take my word for it. The
cherry's gone, nothing left now but the box it came
in."

Angela got the whipping of her life; beat half to
death by an elderly, outraged, Puerto Rican mother
with a teddy bear for a club. If it hadn't hurt so
bad, it might have been funny.

When her mother finally quit there was nothing
left of the bear but a floppy brown rag of cloth. Its
cotton guts lay strewn from one end of the room to
the other.

"Get out of my house," her mother yelled,
"you're no daughter of mine."

"Works for me," Angela said.

She got dressed even as her mother sat on the
edge of the bed, occasionally screaming, "Get out,
whore!"

She grabbed some extra clothes, the money they
had saved, and went out to look for Jimmy.

That was the falling of shit-brick number one.

Brick number two fell when she found Jimmy.
They didn't get married right away ("soon," Jimmy

kept saying), but they did rent an apartment in the sleazy section of the city. And the "friends" he had told her about, the guys from The House, as it was called, came to live with them—at least two of them.

She thought: Now isn't this the shits? I get kicked out of the house with my mother thinking I'm the local amusement ride, and two assholes I never wanted to live with, never wanted to meet, have moved in with me.

There was a positive side. Jimmy told her that there had originally been four assholes.

Thank the Blessed Virgin for small favors.

But the two guys scared her, made her flesh creep around her bones. There was that wild laughing one who was always sniffing glue, "doing the bag" he called it. And then there was Stone, never speaking, just watching with razor-blade eyes that stripped away her clothes and ripped her flesh.

She wanted Jimmy to make them leave, but he wouldn't.

Or it seemed that way at first. After a time she realized it wasn't that he didn't want them to leave, but, like her, he was afraid of them. Their "friendship" had shed its skin to reveal something considerably less tasteful—a kind of cancer that dominated him.

Then came the third shit-brick: Brian Blackwood.

After that, the bricks began to fall like rain.

So, here they were, with Brian and his two crazy pals, parked in the woods, stopping for a while before they . . .

God, she didn't want to think about it.

The things she and Jimmy had seen them do.

The way they killed in cold blood. The way they had . . .

No. She would not think back on it. She could not.

But she did. The candy bars and cold drinks she had eaten for breakfast, lunch and dinner turned to acid and she felt weak. She bent forward and vomited.

When her stomach was empty, she dry-heaved, and after an eternity the spasms stopped.

By the Blessed Virgin, was there no way out of this?

She and Jimmy were caught in a nightmare.

She fastened her pants, adjusted her shirt.

What in God's name were they going to do? There had to be a way out—besides . . . that way. The way Brian would offer them.

She looked back at the car. Brian's white face was still visible.

She couldn't see Jimmy or the others, the shadows in the car were too thick.

But Brian's face was as visible as the full moon on a clear summer night. And when the lightning flashed, it seemed unreal, like some sort of leather mask.

She considered running, but felt if she did they would take it out on Jimmy.

No, she had to go back.

She pushed out of the wet brush and walked back to the car, watching Brian's face all the way.

God, that face, that pasty-white face, looking out of the car at the night.

SIX

The goblins were back; nightmare riders galloping hell-bent for leather through a dismal brainstorm of painful memories. Faces livid with scars, eyes dangling on stalks against cheeks with grey-green complexions.

Becky awoke, balls of sweat the size of BBs ran off her face and breasts, gathered in her pubic thatch. Her nightgown clung to her. Her hair was damp.

She rolled from beneath the covers, careful not to awaken Monty who slept (and she envied this) like a petrified tree. Head in hands, she sat on the edge of the bed and wished she smoked.

After a moment, she got up, found her way to the dark living room. She went to the window, moved the curtains aside, looked out at the lake.

The rain had dried up and left the night-land polished. The lake was calm, glistening with the moon's silver; an almost full moon. Normally, she would have found beauty in it, but not tonight; it reminded her of a dead, bleached eye.

A gentle wind brewed up, came down through the pines, sighed loud enough for her to hear, pushed lightly through the lake and rolled it; shook the windowpane with a noise like dry, rattling bones.

It passed on.

It was cold in the house. Becky shivered. It was as if the scythe of the Reaper had passed over the cabin and spared them, but touched them with its chill.

An image came to her of the scythe swinging back. But the thought did not hold.

She turned her eyes back to the lake, to the short wooden dock sticking out into the water like a dark tongue—like Clyde's tongue when the shirt strips had done their work.

Beads of moisture condensed on the glass, flowed down in mercurylike globs . . . *the color of blood.*

The glass went smoky-dark, like an obsidian mirror. The bloody drops stood out against it in bold relief, oozed down the glass s l o w l y . . .

And then there were the eyes. Huge eyes; like infernal jack-o'-lantern eyes.

And there was a sound; a growling noise like a hungry night beast.

And this beast with the glowing eyes and growling stomach was moving fast toward her, and there were things in its head, things behind the jack-o'-lantern—eyes.

No, it was not a beast, not glowing eyes. It was . . .

Nothing now.

No beads of blood.

No beast or thing that looked like a beast.

Just the wind out there with the pines, the water and the boiled-egg moon.

Becky sagged, stumbled away from the window. She put a hand on the arm of the couch, kept herself from toppling. Her nightgown was damper than ever; shaped around her breasts and pulled up between her legs like a clutching hand—*Clyde's hand*.

God, don't think that. He's dead. He's not some kind of boogeyman.

Or is he? she thought suddenly.

She sat down on the couch and shivered. The room was freezing. She was damp, and there was the icy touch of fear about her.

Get a grip on yourself, old girl. You're starting to go Flip City.

Starting?

After a moment she padded to the kitchen, drank a glass of water.

Goblins, she thought. Why goblins? Why the eyes? The growling?

All of that couldn't have been a dream. No way. It was too graphic, too intense.

Or maybe she was just going Flip City.

No. No, goddamnit, she wasn't flipping. The psychiatrist was full of shit. It was some sort of premonition. A warning. She could feel it in her bones.

She tried to make sense of it all, but it was an impossible task.

Finally she gave it up and went back to bed.

But she slept badly.

SEVEN

October 30, 3:01 A.M.

The others slept for a while. He had promised them rest, all through the night and the next night. It was a long time to wait, and the waiting made his hands itch, but by now they were hunted. If they lay low for the rest of the day and most of tomorrow, things would probably loosen up. The law would most likely think they had made the Louisiana border, and would go looking for them there. That would give them some slack.

Then he could make his move.

Oh yeah, he was clever. It made him smile to think about it. Of course, he had help. He had Clyde inside his head.

But this waiting . . . Man, he was tired of that.

He opened the car door and got out.

It was chilly, but not quite cold. The night had cleared and the moon was highly visible. It was so near full it looked that way at first glance. In a couple of days it would be completely filled out. Doing what he had to do beneath a full moon seemed like a good idea.

He looked around him.

Driving into this pasture, parking on the far side under these trees had been a stroke of genius (he couldn't remember if he had thought of it, or if Clyde had). How were the cops going to check all the pastures in this area? There were hundreds. The odds of them checking this particular one were one in a million. Even by air they couldn't see beneath these trees. It was a perfect spot for the time being.

"What's that?" he said softly. He cocked his head, listened, said, "Yeah, yeah, I know, Clyde. Soon. Real soon."

EIGHT

October 30, 8:23 A.M.

In the morning, the first thing they did was make instant coffee and unpack the box of stale doughnuts they had brought along. When they had eaten, Montgomery said:

"I'm going to drive into Minnanette for some stuff. Want to go?"

Becky smiled. The dreams were less haunting in the daylight, but their chill lingered on.

"No. I'm going to stay here and read my magazines. I brought a whole herd of the buggers."

Montgomery laughed. "All right, you can round up your herd of magazines while I'm gone. But let's make a list of things we need before I go. Anything special?"

"Let's see."

Becky found a pen and paper. They made a list, talking items back and forth, discarding some, seconding others.

"Sure you can find Minnanette?" Becky asked.

"Dean said to hit the blacktop, drive ten miles and don't blink."

"Sounds like Dean."

They kissed at the door. Montgomery thought it was a lot like kissing a dry sponge.

He went out to the Rabbit, backed it around, looked at the cabin in his rearview mirror.

Becky was already inside.

"Swell place," he said, and drove out of there.

When he finished off mile ten, the first thing he saw was a gas station. Or rather a gas station and store combination. There was a big sign above the door that read "Pop's."

Montgomery drove on past to inspect the town. Or was the proper word community? Either sounded like a polite euphemism for the place.

But it was nice. Somehow seemed like a refuge. A small town where time moved slowly and nothing special ever happened.

Then maybe it just seemed like that because he was away from Becky for awhile; away from those caged-animal eyes.

He passed a laundromat with a sign that read "Minnanette Washateria." There was also a post office, a cubicle-sized bank and a sprinkling of stores. Not far from the road were a few houses. Blacktop and clay roads branched off in every direction, probably leading their way past what made up the population of Minnanette, which, according to Dean, was about five hundred. That figure seemed large to Montgomery, but then again, it wouldn't take much of a town to service five hundred people, and from this point, it wasn't too outrageously far to Livingston or Lufkin, and one or both of those places would be where all the serious shopping was done.

He drove a ways and found what served as a school. It was incredibly small, and probably housed all grades.

A little farther on there was only the forest on either side of the road. The tour of Minnanette was complete.

He turned around and drove back to Pop's. That seemed to be the hot spot.

A pickup had parked in front of the gas pumps, and an old man in greasy grey coveralls was putting gas in it when Montgomery pulled up and got out.

For the first time he really noticed the freshness of the air. Galveston always smelled like some giant was airing out a pair of stale underwear in front of a huge fan.

The old man in coveralls turned around and looked at Montgomery. His eyes roaming up and down, tagging him "stranger."

Montgomery nodded at him.

"Right with ya," the old man said.

"No hurry."

A lean brown arm came out of the truck window, handed the old man (Pop?) a wad of bills.

"Get you some change," the old man said. "Right back."

"Okay," a woman said.

Montgomery liked the voice. Lots of country twang with an underlying touch of velvet. Kind of woman who'd drink her whisky straight and roll up with a man and fuck like a snake.

Sex. That was certainly on his mind a lot.

And why not?

There you go again, he told himself. Such a fine, understanding husband you are.

But he still walked around where he could see into the truck.

The woman's face was nice. Large-boned, but attractive. Damned attractive. She didn't wear makeup. Her hair was shoulder-length and brown.

She turned to look at Montgomery.

Her eyes were large, like a doe's. She smiled at him, a sexy, out of the corner of her mouth smile.

Or maybe that was just the way his brain was receiving it. Probably just friendly, nothing more.

She winked.

No, sir, more than friendly.

Montgomery grinned. She was blatant, but effective. And he liked it. Somehow, Becky's inability to accept him sexually made him feel castrated. This looked like a woman who could hang a new set of balls for him.

". . . *never had no balls, Monty. That's what's wrong with you . . .*" His father's voice intruded on his memory. Mad. Very mad because of what he had let Billy Sylvester do to his little brother. It hadn't bothered him so much then, but now that he was grown (taller?), it ate at him. Maybe his old man was right all along. No balls. That was his problem.

To hell with the old man.

He winked back.

She blushed.

That was surprising. Country shy and aggressive too. A weird combination.

Or maybe, he thought with sudden embarrassment, she had merely had something in her eye and he thought she had winked. And he, the big lover, had just made a fool out of himself.

Pop came back with the change. "All right, Marjorie . . ."

He couldn't see her face now, just Pop's back, his grey head.

". . . nine dollars and fifteen cents change."

"Thanks, Pop," she said.

"All right. Come back now."

She pulled out of the driveway and Montgomery watched her go, wondering if he had just made an ass of himself. But then again, it didn't matter. He'd never see her again.

"Now, what can I do for you, young feller?"

Young feller? Just like in the movies, thought Montgomery.

"Need a few things from the store. Little gas, I guess?"

"Little gas'll cost you a lot. Stuff's high as hell. Some folks blame me. Hell, I ain't got nothing to do with it. Do I look like a goddamned Arab to you? I sell it cheap as I can. Any cheaper and I don't make a dime."

"No."

"No what?"

"No, you don't look like a goddamned Arab to me."

Pop laughed. "Sorry. Just get tired of all this gas shit, you know?"

"Yeah."

"You want to pull your car up to the pump? Uh, how much?"

"Fill it."

Montgomery parked the car by the pumps, went inside. The store seemed frozen in a time warp. Merchandise was everywhere. Dangling from nails. Cramped and stacked in corners. Nothing was neatly aisled or arranged. Most everything was covered with a thin skin of dust. A large number of items were derelicts of a distant and simpler time: hair oil was in abundance—all brands, some of which were now defunct—and there was toothpaste so old it had probably soured in the tube, and a cardboard comb display with a logo in the under left-hand corner that read: "5 Cents. Look Your Best!" Only three combs were missing out of a dozen.

"Got some old stuff here, Pop . . . All right if I call you Pop?"

The old man was just coming in the door, wiping his hands on a rag. "What's that?" he said.

"I said you have some old stuff here. It is all right if I call you Pop?"

"Sure, call me most anything, long as you call me for dinner. Car didn't need much, by the way."

"Volkswagens are good on gas."

"Well, nothing personal, but I wouldn't own one of them foreign sonofabitches."

Montgomery smiled. "I said you got some old stuff here."

"Sure do, some of it twenty years old or better."

Pop moved behind a dusty glass counter, sat down on a stool. Montgomery walked over to look at what was beneath the glass. There were plastic fishing flies—most of them sun-faded—and nestled uncharacteristically among the flies was a giant peanut pattie that looked old enough to have been whipped up from the peanut crop of '48.

"You a fisherman?" Pop asked.

"Yes, thought I'd get a bit of line time in today or tomorrow, in fact."

"Here." Pop reached under the counter, brought out one of the flies. "Try this. They don't make them anymore, some reason or another, but they sure used to bring in the fish. I still got one and I'm still catching fish on it. Here, take it, you can have it."

"That's kind of you."

"Not really. Nobody is going to buy this shit anyway."

"Well," Montgomery said, slipping the fly in his pocket, "I hope no one buys that peanut pattie anyway."

Pop laughed. "Wouldn't let nobody buy that sonofabitch. Talk about knocking your dick in the dirt. That thing is as old as I am, and that ain't thirty-nine, friend."

Montgomery smiled.

"New around here?" Pop asked.

"Kinda . . . I mean we aren't permanent. Just vacationing. Friends, Eva and Dean Beaumont, loaned us a cabin down by the lake."

"Yeah, I know the Beaumonts. They come down here just about every summer. That Beaumont feller likes to talk fishing."

"That he does."

"You know, pretty soon, won't be nothing but goddamned cabins down by that lake. All of them built by city folks trying to get a whiff of clean air. No offense."

"None taken."

"You from Galveston too, like your friends?"

"Yeah."

"I hear the fucking ocean out there isn't nothing but a damned oil slick anymore. That right?"

"Afraid so. Mostly anyway."

"Damn cities. I hate the sonofabitches. They bleed the man right out of a feller. No offense."

"None taken." Not too much anyway, Monty thought.

"Like that goddamned Houston. Bastard's too

close for me. All that killing and such. It's gonna spread, like some kind of goddamned disease. Be at our back door before long."

"There are a lot of people who like it. Houston, not the killing."

"God knows why. It's a fucking sewer . . . You want a basket to push around? There's some at the back of the store . . . Damn cities and newfangled shit, that's why I let the peanut pattie rot."

"Somehow, I don't see the connection."

"Damn thing may be old and rotten, but it reminds me of a time when a man could eat cheaper and a man's handshake was better than ten contracts and all the courts in the land. Reminds me of a time when I could sit on my front porch and not worry about getting my ears shot off by some crazy. Hell, I don't even feel safe out here in the sticks anymore."

"Times change, Pop."

"That supposed to be an answer for all this shit?"

"Guess not."

Montgomery walked to the rear of the store, pulled out one of the three shopping carts. Above them, hanging on nails, were two rows of Halloween masks; grotesque things. A handful of them were the pull-over latex kind; he'd always wanted one as a kid.

He leaned forward and examined the masks. They were pretty gruesome, all right. One was nothing but a skull face with rubbery sprigs of hair on the crown. The others were a bit more elaborate. The most elaborate was one with a knife (rubber, of course) sticking in the forehead. A purply blotch of blood flowed down across the contorted face.

"Hey, Pop, these masks old?"

Pop looked up. "No. Three Halloweens back, I guess. Why? You thinking of going tricker-treatin' tomorrow night?"

"Maybe. But I won't stop here. Afraid you might give me that peanut pattie."

Pop whooped at that. "Hell, boy, it's so damned old it don't even stink anymore."

"Just the same . . ."

Pop cackled.

Montgomery pushed the cart, put a loaf of bread in it.

"Hey, son?"

"Yeah." Montgomery put a can of green beans in the cart.

"That gal, the one in the truck, Marjorie. She looks pretty good, don't she?"

Montgomery could feel heat bubbling up through his body, filling to the top of his skull. It wasn't passion. It was guilt. "Yeah, she looked all right."

"All right, hell! If I was a little younger, and not happily married—well, maybe if I was just a little younger—I'd hustle that little old gal . . . Come to think of it, I'd have to be a lot younger. Used to wake up every morning with a hard-on. These mornings I do good to wake up."

Montgomery began to push the cart faster. He was suddenly anxious to be through shopping and get back to Becky. For some reason he felt uneasy away from her.

Guilt maybe, he thought. Looking for women in pickup trucks to satisfy my deprived sex urges. Just the sort of thing I said I'd never do.

Face up to it, No Balls Monty. Becky needs time,

patience and love. You think you've offered that?
Do you?

No way, José. You've just given the impression,
set a stage play for yourself. Always trying to weasel
out of your responsibilities, find the easy path.

"... *never had no balls, Monty. That's what's
wrong with you. No balls.*"

"... *sorry, son, about your wife* ... *She's been
raped* ..."

"... *had been home, Officer, I might have done
something. It might not have happened.*" (Sure.)

"... *wish to sign as a Conscientious Objector?*"

"... *I do.*"

"... *opposed to violence of any kind?*"

"*I am.*"

"... *would not raise a hand to protect your
home?*"

"... *could not kill another human being.*"

"... *never had no balls* ..."

Thoughts. Words. His brother's face. Billy Sylvester smiling, taking his lunch money ... using a
candy wrapper off the yard to pick up dogshit ...
"*Smile when he eats it, pussy.*" His own face.
Smiling an insane Sardonicus grin. Piss running
down his leg.

All the images of the past, all the terrors and
fears and excuses of a lifetime came tumbling out of
Montgomery's subconscious and rolled down the
stairs of his memory and came to rest in an uncere-
monious heap.

He was trembling when he put the last items in
the cart and rolled it to the checkout counter.

"You okay, son?" Pop asked. "You look peaked."

"Coming down with
(*the lack of balls blues*)
some kind of cold probably."

"Time of year for it. Weather changes so damn much. Rain one minute, dry the next. Cold then warm."

"How much?"

"Let's see." Pop tallied it up on an ancient cash register. "Thirty dollars and twenty-three cents . . . don't take no checks from outa town. Nothing personal."

"Understand." Montgomery took out his wallet, gave Pop three tens, dug the change from his pants pocket.

Montgomery took the bags, one under each arm, and started out.

"Come back."

"Will do."

On the way to his car he thought: Why have all these things so long buried, all these fears, suddenly come out of their graves to rattle their chains? What's with all this internal conflict? It was as if it had lain in ambush all this time, waiting for a good time to strike. To hit him while he was down.

Well, he wasn't going to let stupid, insane fears from the subconscious ruin his life. This was the twentieth century. Man was civilized and no longer needed to carry a big club and beat his chest and spurt his enemy's blood.

My God, just a few years back there had been Woodstock. The Age of Aquarius. A time of social enlightenment.

And a time of wars, riot and hate.

And let's not forget that not too long back a nasty little personal thing happened. Your wife got raped.

All right, all right, it happened. It's bad. We'll get over it. But what can I do besides comfort and help Becky along? Christ, I'm not a caped crusader. I'm just an ordinary man whose wife was unlucky enough to get raped. That's all, I'm just unlucky . . .

And a coward.

"*. . . never had no balls, Monty.*"

Montgomery put the groceries in the back of the Rabbit and got in. The old man, Pop, was standing outside the store with an RC in his hand, leaning against the building, sipping slowly, watching.

Does he know I'm a coward? Can you smell it on a person? Is there truly such a thing as the smell of fear?

Montgomery cranked up the car, looked back at Pop and smiled. The old man lifted his RC in friendly salute.

Waving at Pop, Montgomery pulled onto the blacktop, not looking back to see if the old man had returned the gesture.

A chill shook him, seeped down to the very core of his existence. With a twist of his shoulders, he tried to throw it off, but it remained.

You're going crackers, he thought. Crackers. You're not responsible for what happened. You weren't there. If you had been, things might have been different.

(clear as a bell, the vision of Billy Sylvester smashing the dog turd in his brother's face)

might not have happened.

All blood under the bridge now. Forget it.

Said softly to himself: "There is nothing to fear. Nothing to fear. Nothing to fear at all."

But the chill did not leave him.

NINE

Becky read *Cosmopolitan* all of five minutes before she tossed it against the wall. Its pages fluttered noisily and colorfully before striking the floor like a dead bird.

Once, that magazine of near-exposed breasts, chic fashion and advice had seemed so mature, worldly, modern and entertaining. Now it seemed little more than a three-hundred-page advertisement for sex and its trappings.

Sex.

If there was one thing she was not interested in, it was sex. No, thank you very much, it's yucky, get it off my plate. No, she was dead to that. Did not want any man touching her body in any manner—friendly or otherwise. Even Monty's hands, once familiar travelers on her personal terrain, seemed to crawl over her flesh like slimy worms. His body, close to her at night while they slept, the touch of it was reptilian or rather what the word had come to represent, something repulsive, frightening and evil.

She wondered if her repugnance to Monty's touch was merely because of the rape, an act of man, a gender to which he belonged. Or was it something deeper? Some bacterialike culture that had existed all along and was just now at the height of its gestation. His cowardice? Could it be that?

Had the rape caused her to look at Monty in a new light?

She had grown up in a "sophisticated" environment; grown up thinking the measure of a man was not in the bulge of his bicep or the heat of his temper. And certainly that still held true. But perhaps this modern concept sometimes went too far, was used by men like Monty to cover up their weaknesses. The old "I've got nothing to prove" might have an addition, "and I'm glad of it, because I'm scared to death."

Grinning to herself, she thought: If my old sociology professor (also Monty's) could hear me now. He'd label me a cultural throwback, a sociological retard.

Yet, why had she cheered when she'd read about a woman and her children being attacked by three men in broad daylight (even while a large number of "modern men" watched) and along comes this 240-pound truck driver who immediately attacked all three bare-handed?

Cheered even more when she read that he had broken the arm of one. Ruptured another. Shattered the last one's jaw.

All this while a group of "modern men," "civilized men," had watched in gape-jawed stupidity.

She made herself a cup of instant coffee and tried to put such thoughts out of her mind. She was being far too harsh on Monty and she knew it. But she knew that at the bottom of it all, there was more than just a little truth to her feelings.

After a few sips of the coffee, she realized that it was not what she had wanted after all. She looked out the window. It was beautiful. The day was turning out fine. October and seventy degrees, and it had been fairly chilly just an hour ago.

It wasn't going to be a day for worry and introspection. It was a day to be outside, to be warmed by the rays of the sun.

She poured the coffee in the sink, went back to pick up the *Cosmopolitan*, straightened its damaged pages, placed it on the table and went outside.

A gentle wind blew across the lake, billowed her loose sweatshirt and baggy pants (she had not been able to wear anything tight since the rape; reminded her too much of her sexuality, made her feel vulnerable), whipped her hair.

There were a lot of birds about, flittering from one tree to another, chirping, celebrating the warmth of a late fall day.

There was a squirrel out by the little storage house, quietly nibbling on something, but keeping a wary eye on Becky's progress.

Becky stooped to one knee, made a clucking sound at the squirrel and held out her hand, absently running thumb and forefinger together.

The squirrel wasn't having any of that shit. It hadn't stopped its nibbling, but it was giving Becky a suspicious eye.

Becky rose to a half-crouch, moved toward the squirrel, still making the clucking noise, still working thumb and forefinger together.

The squirrel allowed her to get within six feet before turning and darting up a pine, the morsel still in its mouth. Halfway up the tree it stopped, leaned out, held only by its remarkable claws, and looked down. It made a sudden chittering sound, then, like a jet, it was gone; a brown flash lost among evergreen pine needles.

Becky smiled wryly. Smart little bastard, aren't you? Well, have it your way.

She turned, started back toward the house, but stopped at the shed. Exploring its interior just might give her something to do, something to keep her mind off things. Eva had said there was a key hidden in a magnetic key box, attached beneath the metal steps. She had told Becky that there was fishing equipment and tools stored in there. Neither were particularly interesting to her, but it was something to do.

Becky groped beneath the steps for the key box.

"gonna cut her cunt out . . ."

She stood upright. What the hell was that? Oh God, not again. She could feel the sweat running down her face and neck. Oh please

". . . ram it all the way up her ass . . ."

not again.

She stood with her teeth clenched, silence inside her head.

The pines whispered. The lake gurgled. She bent once again to the steps, found the key box. Put the rusted key in the lock

". . . wanta be first . . ."

turned it, pulled the lock loose

". . . up her ass . . ."

and went inside. The tin shed was hot, cluttered. There were a few tools: hoes, shovels, an axe, a hammer, a saw. There were some long plastic rod and reel cases hung on the wall. That made her think of something Dean had said:

"It's isolated up there, but people around those parts are honest. Why, we've had that stuff up there for the past three years. Safe as it can be. Wouldn't be nothing to snapping that old rusty padlock if they took a mind to."

For some reason she could not explain, that memory struck a note of fear in her, something important that she couldn't quite put together. It was all too vague . . . too symbolic.

"*. . . ram it all the way up her ass . . .*"

In the corner of the shed she saw something she couldn't quite put a name to, but it was familiar

"*. . . ram it . . .*"

her brother had owned one of those awful things, back when she lived in Gladewater. She could remember them taunting her with it, and with what they had collected between its metal jaws. It was a frog gig. A spring-cocked device that snapped

"*. . . all the way up her ass . . .*"

together on an unsuspecting frog—a device for acquiring frog legs. In the case of her brother, a device for inflicting torture on the harmless creatures . . . and then using it to chase her around, sometimes with the poor frog still squirming between the sharp claws, struggling with painful futility.

"*. . . isolated up there . . .*"

She backed out of the shed as if the gig were something alive. The mere sight of it

"*. . . up her ass . . .*"

made her want to vomit. Trembling, she replaced the padlock and returned the key to the box beneath the steps, got away from there quick.

She turned toward the lake, walked out to the dock, hoping somehow the sight of the calm lake would calm her as well.

Potpourri thoughts gathered, flapped like bats in her skull. She could not shake them.

"*. . . cut her cunt out . . .*"

"*. . . all the way up . . .*"

"*. . . be first . . .*"

"*. . . isolated up there . . .*"

"... *all the way up her ass* ..."

Becky sat down on the dock suddenly, placed her hands over her ears.

No good. Voices bounced around in her head; racquetball game of voices.

Images now:

Dock gone. Lake gone. Trees gone. Sky turning dark.

She stood in darkness, alone, among the pines. No! Not alone. *Something was there with her.* Shadows. Shadows that moved among the tree trunks, scuffled across the dry leaves and rust-colored pine needles.

She was running. The shadows were running after her.

The lake ... she could see the lake. And then something horrible jumped in front of her.

Daylight winked in. Nighttime winked out.

She was lying on her back on the dock. Above her, cotton-candy clouds raced between the green tips of the pines that grew by the lake.

She sat up, looked out over the water. Her body shook. Her mouth was dry.

Slowly, it was going away. Images less than shadows now. But there was a sound, the hungry animal growl she heard last night.

And then it died inside her head.

Birds chirped. The water lapped. The wind sighed.

Then she heard the sound again, outside her head, entering the skull through the ears.

For a moment fear possessed her, then it died like a broken fever.

She recognized that sound. It wasn't like the one that had been in her head, it was a familiar sound, the sewing-machine hum of the Rabbit.

Tires crunched in the drive. The motor stopped. A door opened.

At a run, Becky went to meet Monty, tears streaming down her face, and for the time being, the thought of his arms was not so repulsive.

TEN

From the October 30 edition of the *Galveston News*, page 1.

COUPLE MURDERED

Mr. Dean Beaumont and his wife, Eva Beaumont, were found murdered in their home at 7501½ Heard's Lane this morning. The bodies were discovered by police when Mr. Beaumont's employer, Ball High School, reported Mr. Beaumont absent from work, and not responding to phone calls. Police discovered the bodies shortly after 9 a.m. The bodies were found in the bedroom and both had been mutilated beyond immediate and positive

identification. The motive for
the murders has not been determined, though robbery is
suspected. No missing items
were verified, however.
There was a considerable
amount of vandalism. Paint-
ings had been smashed over a
bedpost and blood from the
victims had been poured into
a flower vase. The next-door
neighbors reported that they
had heard nothing out of the
ordinary. The couple had
been dead for at least twelve
hours . . .

At this point, no one knew there was a connection between the two savaged bodies and what was
going to happen to Montgomery and Becky Jones.

ELEVEN

Later that night, while highway patrolmen and
local law officers searched for the car Trawler had
identified before he was murdered, the kids continued to sit in the pasture and while away the hours
eating candy bars and drinking hot Cokes.

And Becky lay in her bed and dreamed:

Shadows moved from behind the pines. Faces burst into the glow of the moon—goblin faces.

Laughter.

"*I wanta ram it all the way up her ass.*"

More darkness.

Moonlight.

Darkness.

Alternating slats of each.

A body, dangling, upside down; a woman, her feet attached to something . . . something Becky could not define.

The shoulder-length hair was dark and undulated with the breeze. Blood dripped from the face, congealed in the hair, splattered the ground. The face . . . she couldn't see the face, but it seemed to be turning, like the earth orbiting the sun, turning, so slow, but turning, half-profile . . . the face was a mess. Hair was plastered to it with blood. There was a deep, dark crack in the skull. The face was turning even more . . . looking like . . .

NO!

Becky awoke. Sat upright in bed. The face had looked like . . . Oh God, could it have been?

Monty was awake. He turned to her. "What's wrong, hon?"

"What's always wrong? The dreams . . . the premonitions."

"Just nightmares—"

"Fuck you!"

She pulled away from him, rolled over on her side and closed her eyes. But she did not try to sleep. She did not want to sleep. Did not want to see the rest of that face, for she feared whose face it might be.

Monty called to her once, softly.

She did not answer.

He sighed, rolled over and tugged at the bed-clothes. Soon she could hear the sound of regular breathing. He was asleep.

Good, that was what she wanted, to be left alone. Or was it?

Oh God, she did and she didn't. She wanted to be alone and she never wanted to be alone. One moment it was comfortable, the next it was if she were on the face of the moon looking out at earth, thousands of lonely miles away.

Today when Monty held her on the dock after the premonition, it had been wonderful. The love and concern he felt for her had radiated from him as warmly as the sun, so why now, when he was merely expressing his concern, should she be so angry with him?

What if things were reversed? It was him telling her that he was having premonitions. Would she believe him?

She wondered.

And who says the dreams are premonitions? she asked herself. What dream have you had that has come true other than the first?

Perhaps the doctor was right, it's all in your head and the first dream was nothing more than a coincidence, wishful thinking.

It was possible.

Even likely.

After a while, Becky rolled over gently and looked at Monty. He slept clutching the pillow to his cheek. She reached out and stroked his hair.

Why can't we touch? Really touch? Why can't we?

No answers came to her. She rolled away from

him and stared into the darkness, willing away sleep.

But it came anyway, this time without dreams.

Until just before morning, then she had a very ugly one.

TWELVE

October 31, 12:02 A.M.

The blond kid driving the '66 Chevy through the velvet night was named Brian Blackwood. He had the Chevy vent glass cranked all the way open and the wind was blasting his hair back. His eyes were watered with tears, but they were not tears of remorse, sadness or pain; they were fostered by the cool October wind and the rapid movement of the car. There was no room left inside Brian for idle tears, not anymore. From here on out he was a rock, and a rock felt no pain.

The waiting had gotten to him. He wanted to push on, get to the task at hand.

But he knew that wasn't wise. If he could lay low one more night, the law would pretty much be through with the area and things would be safe.

Yet, the waiting was eating at him, and the voice in his head was persistent. He had decided to change locations, find a place a little closer to their destination. Camp there. Just being closer would help ease the pain in his head.

He mentally visualized the map he had made
Dean Beaumont draw; it was clearly outlined in his
head, and he no longer needed to look at it, even if
he was making his way there by roundabout meth-
ods.

Soon . . . Soon . . . Soon.

In the last few days he had witnessed three
murders, contributed to all three, and personally
performed one himself (he could still visualize the
deep, red arc he had made in her throat shortly
after slicing the nipples from her breasts). He hated
that the highway cop had not been his kill, but that
was unavoidable. Looney Tunes had the shotgun,
and it was only fair.

Still, kicking a dead cop in the balls didn't do
much for his disposition; didn't squelch the desire
to kill; a thing that had become like an itch with
him. (Thank you, Clyde, for the rash, because it
feels so good to scratch.)

Soon, tomorrow night, he would scratch that itch
again. He had two murders planned—no, let's be
accurate about this: executions. But before these
executions took place, the victims would know
fear. They would suffer the torment Clyde suffered
waiting in his cell. Thinking about those grey walls
and steel bars . . . And they would feel much more
pain than he felt when he hung himself.

Why, Clyde? Why? Not like you to do that sort of
thing.

Ah, but maybe there is a why. Is that you I feel
stomping about in the back of my brain, Clyde? Is
that your mind mating with my mind, possessing
my soul with your own? Are you me? Am I you?

Huh?

Oh yeah, I hear you, baby, I hear you, and they'll

get theirs soon. Forgive my doubts about you. I'm tired, and it's so weird.

What?

Tomorrow night. No later. I promise.

And so for a few more miles the car rolled on. Brian driving with his pale face ghostlike in the night, the others sleeping, storing up.

PART TWO:
The Guts of the Fish

One year earlier (October to October)

"Some of our neighborhood kids will shoot you for a buck or maybe just for laughs. It's got me so I'm scared to walk my own turf after dark, and I'm pretty tough. But they're real monsters, some of them. And they come younger every year."
—Anonymous Chicago car thief

pos·sessed adj. 2. Controlled by or as by a spirit or force.
—The American Heritage Dictionary

Houses are like the human beings who inhabit them.
—Victor Hugo

(1)

BOYS WILL BE BOYS

ONE

Not so long ago, about a year back, a very rotten kid named Clyde Edson walked the earth. He was street-mean and full of savvy and he knew what he wanted and got it any way he wanted.

He lived in a big, evil house on a dying, grey street in Galveston, Texas, and he collected to him, like an old lady who brings in cats half-starved and near-eaten with mange, the human refuse and the young discards of a sick society.

He molded them. He breathed life into them. He made them feel they belonged. They were his creations, but he did not love them. They were just things to be toyed with until the paint wore thin and the batteries ran down, then out they went.

And this is the way it was until he met Brian Blackwood.

Things got worse after that.

TWO

—guy had a black leather jacket and dark hair combed back virgin-ass tight, slicked down with enough grease to lube a bone-dry Buick; came down the hall walking slow, head up, ice-blue eyes working like acid on everyone in sight; had the hall nearly to himself, plenty of room for his slow-stroll-swagger. The other high school kids were shouldering the wall, shedding out of his path like frenzied snakes shedding out of their skins.

You could see this Clyde was bad news. Hung in time. Fifties-looking. Out of step. But who's going to say, "Hey, dude, you look funny"?

Tough, this guy. Hide like the jacket he wore. No books under his arm, nothing at all. Just cool.

Brian was standing at the water fountain when he first saw him, sipping water, just blowing time between classes; thinking about nothing until along came Clyde, and suddenly he found himself attracted to him. Not in a sexual way. He wasn't funny. But in the manner metal shavings are attracted to a magnet—can't do a thing about it, just got to go to it and cling.

Brian knew who Clyde was, but this was the first time he'd ever been close enough to feel the heat. Before, the guy'd been a tough greaser in a leather jacket who spent most of his time expelled from school. Nothing more.

But now he saw for the first time that the guy had something; something that up close shone like a well-honed razor in the noonday sun.

Cool. He had that.

Class. He had that.

Difference. He had that.

He was a walking power plant.

Name was Clyde. Ol', mean, weird, don't-fuck-with-me Clyde.

"You looking at something?" Clyde growled.

Brian just stood there, one hand resting on the water fountain.

After a while he said innocently: "You."

"That right?"

"Uh-huh."

"Staring at me?"

"I guess."

"I see."

And then Clyde was on Brian, had him by the hair, jerking his head down, driving a knee into his face. Brian went back seeing constellations. Got kicked in the ribs then. Hit in the eye as he leaned forward from that. Clyde was making a regular bop bag out of him.

He hit Clyde back, aimed a nose shot through a swirling haze of colored dots.

And it hurt so good. Like when he made that fat pig Betty Sue Flowers fingernail his back until he bled; thrust up her hips until his cock ached and the rotten-fish smell of her filled his brain . . . Only this hurt better. Ten times better.

Clyde wasn't expecting that. This guy was coming back like he liked it.

Clyde dug that.

He kicked Brian in the nuts, grabbed him by the hair and slammed his forehead against the kid's

nose. Made him bleed good, but didn't get a good
enough lick in to break it.

Brian went down, grabbed Clyde's ankle, bit
it.

Clyde yowled, drug Brian around the hall.

The students watched, fascinated. Some wanted
to laugh at what was happening, but none dared.

Clyde used his free foot to kick Brian in the face.
That made Brian let go . . . for a moment. He dove
at Clyde, slammed the top of his head into Clyde's
bread basket, carried him back against the wall
crying loudly, "Motherfucker!"

Then the principal came, separated them,
screamed at them, and Clyde hit the principal and
the principal went down and now Clyde and Brian
were both standing up, together, *kicking the goddamned shit out of the goddamned principal in the
middle of the goddamned hall.* Side by side they
stood. Kicking. One. Two. Three. One. Two. Three.
Left leg. Right leg. Feet moving together like the
legs of a scurrying centipede . . .

THREE

They got some heat slapped on them for that;
juvenile court action. It was a bad scene.

Brian's mother sat at a long table with his lawyer
and whined like a blender on whip.

Good old mom. She was actually good for something. She had told the judge: "He's a good boy,

your honor. Never got in any trouble before. Probably wouldn't have gotten into this, but he's got no father at home to be an example . . . ," and so forth.

If it hadn't been to his advantage, he'd have been disgusted. As it was, he sat in his place with his nice clean suit and tried to look ashamed and a little surprised at what he had done. And in a way he was surprised.

He looked over at Clyde. He hadn't bothered with a suit. He had his jacket and jeans on. He was cleaning his fingernails with a fingernail clipper.

When Mrs. Blackwood finished, Judge Lowry yawned. It was going to be one of those days. He thought: the dockets are full, this Blackwood kid has no priors, looks clean-cut enough, and this other little shit has a bookful . . . Yet, he is a kid, and I feel big-hearted. Or to put this into perspective, there's enough of a backlog without adding this silly case to it.

If I let the Blackwood kid go, it'll look like favoritism because he's clean-cut and this is his first time—and that is good for something. Yet, if I don't let the Edson kid go too, then I'm saying the same crime is not as bad when its committed by a clean-cut kid with a whining momma.

All right, he thought. We'll keep it simple. Let them both go, but give it all some window dressing.

And it was window dressing, nothing more. Brian was put on light probation, and Clyde, who was already on probation, was given the order to report to his probation officer more frequently, and that was the end of that.

Piece of cake.

The school expelled them for the rest of the

term, but that was no mean thing. They were back on the streets before the day was out.

For the moment, Clyde went his way and Brian went his.

But the bond was formed.

FOUR

A week later, mid-October

Brian Blackwood sat in his room, his head full of pleasant but overwhelming emotions. He got a pen and loose-leaf notebook out of his desk drawer, began to write savagely.

I've never kept a journal before, and I don't know if I'll continue to keep one after tonight, but the stuff that's going on inside of me is boiling up something awful and I feel if I don't get it out I'm going to explode and there isn't going to be anything left of me but blood and shit stains on the goddamned wall.

In school I read about this writer who said he was like that, and if he could write down what was bothering him, what was pushing his skull from the inside, he could find relief, so I'm going to try that and hope for the best, because I've got to tell somebody, and I sure as hell can't tell Mommy-dear this, not that I can really tell her anything, but I've got to let this out of me and I only wish that I could write faster, put it down as fast as I can think.

This guy, Clyde Edson, he's really different and he's changed my life and I can feel it, I know it, it's down in my guts, squirming around like some kind of cancer, eating at me from the inside out, changing me into something new and fresh.

Being around Clyde is like being next to pure power, yeah, like that. Energy comes off of him in waves that nearly knock you down, and it's almost as if I'm absorbing that energy, and like maybe Clyde is sucking something out of me, something he can use, and the thought of that, of me giving Clyde something, whatever it is, makes me feel strong and whole. I mean, being around Clyde is like touching evil, or like that sappy Star Wars shit about being seduced by the Dark Side of The Force, or some such fucking malarky. But you see, this seduction by the Dark Side, it's a damn good fuck, a real jism-spurter, kind that makes your eyes bug, your back pop and your asshole pucker.

Maybe I don't understand this yet, but I think it's sort of like this guy I read about once, this philosopher whose name I can't remember, but who said something about becoming a Superman. Not the guy with the cape. I'm not talking comic book, do-gooder crap here, I'm talking the real palooka. Can't remember just what he said, but from memory of what I read, and from the way I feel now, I figure that Clyde and I are two of the chosen, the Supermen of now, this moment, mutants for the future. I see it sort of like this: man was once a wild animal type that made right by the size of his muscles and not by no bullshit government and laws. Time came when he had to become civilized to survive all the other hardnoses, but now that time has passed 'cause most of the hardnoses have died off and there isn't anything left but a bunch of fucking pussies who couldn't find their ass with a road map or figure how to wipe it without a blueprint. But you see, the mutations are happening again. New survivors are being born, and instead of that muck scientists say we crawled out of in the first place, we're crawling out of this mess the pussies have created with all their human rights shit and laws to protect the weak. Only this time, it isn't like before. Man might have crawled out of that slime to escape the sharks of the sea back then, but this time it's the goddamned sharks that are crawling out and we're mean sonofabitches with razor-sharp teeth and hides like fresh-dug gravel. And most different of all, there's a single-mindedness about us that just won't let up.

I don't know if I'm saying this right, it's not all clear in my head and it's hard to put into words, but I can feel it, goddamnit, I can feel it. Time has come when we've become too civilized, overpopulated, so evolution has taken care of that, it's created a social mutation—Supermen like Clyde and me.

Clyde, he's the raw stuff, sewer sludge. He gets what he wants because he doesn't let anything stand in the way of what he wants, nothing. God, the conversations we had the last couple of days . . . See now, lost my train of thought . . . Oh yeah, the social mutations.

You see, I thought I was some kind of fucking freak all this time. But what it is, I'm just new, different. I mean, from as far back as I can remember, I've been different. I just don't react the way other people do, and I didn't understand why. Crying over dead puppies and shit like that. Big

*fucking deal. Dog's dead, he's dead. What the fuck
do I care? It's the fucking dog that's dead, not me,
so why should I be upset?*

I mean, I remember this little girl next door that
had this kitten when we were kids. She was always
cooing and petting that little mangy bastard. And
one day my Dad—that was before he got tired of
the Old Lady's whining and ran off, and good
riddance, I say—sent me out to mow the yard. He
had this thing about the yard being mowed, and he
had this thing about me doing it. Well, I'm out there
mowing it, and there's that kitten, wandering
around in our yard. Now, I was sick of that kitten,
Mr. Journal, so I picked it up and petted it, went to
the garage and got myself a trowel. I went out in the
front yard and dug a nice deep hole and put that
kitten in it, all except the head, I left that sticking
up. I patted the dirt around its neck real tight, then I
went back and got the lawn mower, started it and
began pushing it toward that little fucking cat. I
could see its head twisting and it started moving its
mouth—meowing, but I couldn't hear it, though I
wish I could have—and I pushed the mower
slowlike toward it, watching the grass chute from
time to time, making sure the grass was really
coming out of there in thick green blasts, and then
I'd look up and see that kitten. When I got a few feet
from it, I noticed that I was on a hard. I mean, I had
a pecker you could have used for a cold chisel.

When I was three feet away, I started to push that
thing at a trot, and when I hit that cat, what a
sound, and I had my eye peeled on that mower
chute, and for a moment there was green and then
there was red with the green and hunks of ragged
grey fur, spewing out, twisting onto the lawn.

Far as I knew, no one ever knew what I did. I just covered up the stump of the cat's neck real good and went on about my business. Later that evening when I was finishing up, the little shit next door came home and I could hear her calling out, "Kitty, kitty, kitty," it was all I could do not to fall down behind the mower laughing. But I kept a straight face, and when she came over and asked if I'd seen Morris— can you get that, Morris?—I said, "No, I'm sorry, I haven't," and she doesn't even get back to her house before she's crying and calling for that little fucking cat again.

Ah, but so much for amusing sidelights, Mr. Journal. I guess the point I'm trying to make is people get themselves tied up and concerned with the damnedest things, dogs and cats, stuff like that. I've yet to come across a dog or cat with a good, solid idea.

God, it feels good to say what I want to say for a change, and to have someone like Clyde who not only understands, but agrees, sees things the same way. Feels good to realize why all the Boy Scout good deed shit never made me feel diddlyshit. Understand now why the good grades and being called smart never thrilled me either. Was all bullshit, that's why. We Supermen don't go for that petty stuff, doesn't mean dick to us. Got no conscience 'cause a conscience isn't anything but a bullshit tool to make you a goddamned pussy, a candy-ass coward. We do what we want, as we please, when we want. I got this feeling that there are more and more like Clyde and me, and in just a little more time, we new ones will rule. And those who are born like us won't feel so out of step, because they'll know by then that the way they feel is okay, and that this is a dog eat dog world full of fucking red, raw meat, and there won't be any bullshit, pussy talk from them, they'll just go out and find that meat and eat it.

These new ones aren't going to be like the rest of the turds who have a clock to tell them when to get up in the morning, a boss that tells them what to do all day and a wife to nag them into doing it to keep her happy lest she cut off the pussy supply. No, no more of that. That old dog ain't going to hunt no more. From then on it'll be every man for himself, take what you want, take the pussy you want, whatever. What a world that would be, a world where every sonofabitch on the block is as mean as a junkyard dog. Every day would be an adventure, a constant battle of muscle and wits.

Oh man, the doors that Clyde has opened for me. He's something else. Just a few days ago I felt like I was some kind of freak hiding out in this world, then along comes Clyde and I find out that the freaks are plentiful, but the purely sane, like Clyde and me, are far and few—least right now. Oh yeah, that Clyde . . . it's not because he's so smart, either. Least not in a book-learned sense. The thing that impresses me about him is the fact that he's so raw and ready to bite, to just take life in his teeth and shake that motherfucker until the shit comes out.

Me and Clyde are like two halves of a whole. I'm blond and fair, intelligent, and he's dark, short and muscular, just able to read. I'm his gears and he's my oil, the stuff that makes me run right. We give to each other . . . What we give is . . . Christ, this will sound screwy, Mr. Journal, but the closest I can come to describing it is psychic energy. We feed off each other.

Jesus fucking H. Christ, starting to ramble. But feel better. That writer's idea must be working because I feel drained. Getting this out is like having been constipated for seventeen years of my life, and suddenly I've taken a laxative and I've just shit the biggest turd that can be shit by man, bear or elephant, and it feels so goddamned good, I want to yell to the skies.

Hell, I've had it. Feel like I been on an all-night fuck with a nympho on Spanish Fly. Little later Clyde's supposed to come by, and I'm going out the window, going with him to see The House. He's told me about it, and it sounds really fine. He says he's going to show me some things I've never seen before. Hope so.

Damn, it's like waiting to be blessed with some sort of crazy, magical power or something. Like being given the ability to strike people with leprosy or wish Raquel Welch up all naked and squirming on the rack and you with a dick as long and hard and hot as a heated poker, and her looking up at you and yelling for you to stick it to her before she cums just looking at you. Something like that, anyway.

Well, won't be long now and Clyde will be here. Guess I need to go sit over by the window, Mr. Journal, so I won't miss him. If Mom finds me missing after a while, things could get a little sticky, but I doubt she'll report her only, loving son to the parole board. Would be tacky. I always just tell her I'll be moving out just as soon as I can get me a job, and that shuts her up. Christ, she acts like she's in love with me or something, isn't natural.

Enough of this journal shit. Bring on the magic, Clyde.

FIVE

Two midnight shadows seemed to blow across the yard of the Blackwood home. Finally, those shadows broke out of the overlapping darkness of the trees, hit the moonlight and exploded into two teenagers: Clyde and Brian, running fast and hard. Their heels beat a quick, sharp rhythm on the sidewalk, like the too-fast ticking of clocks; timepieces from the Dark Side, knocking on toward a gruesome destiny.

After a moment the running stopped. Doors slammed. A car growled angrily. Lights burst on, and the black '66 sailed away from the curb. It sliced down the quiet street like a razor being drawn across a vein, cruised between dark houses where only an occasional light burned behind a window like a fearful gold eye gazing through a contact lens.

A low-slung, yellow dog making its nightly trash-can route crossed the street, fell into the Chevy's headlights.

The car whipped for the dog, but the animal was fast and lucky and only got its tail brushed before making the curb.

A car door flew open in a last attempt to bump the dog, but the dog was too far off the street. The car bounced up on the curb briefly, then whipped back onto the pavement.

The dog was gone now, blending into the darkness of a tree-shadowed yard.

The door slammed and the motor roared loudly. The car moved rapidly off into the night, and from its open windows, carried by the wind, came the high, wild sound of youthful laughter.

SIX

The House, as Clyde called it, was just below Stoker Street, just past where it intersected King, not quite bookended between the two streets, but nearby, on a more narrow one. And there it waited.

Almost reverently, like a hearse that has arrived to pick up the dead, the black '66 Chevy entered the drive, parked.

Clyde and Brian got out, stood looking up at the house for a moment, considering it as two monks would a shrine.

Brian felt a sensation of trembling excitement, and though he would not admit it, a tinge of fear.

The House was big, old, grey and ugly. It looked gothic, out of step with the rest of the block. Like something out of Poe or Hawthorne. It crouched like a falsely obedient dog. Upstairs two windows showed light, seemed like cold, rectangular eyes considering prey.

The moon was bright enough that Brian could see the dead grass in the yard, the dead grass in all the yards down the block. It was the time of year for dead grass, but to Brian's way of thinking, this grass looked browner, deader. It was hard to imagine it ever being alive, ever standing up tall and bright and green.

The odd thing about The House was the way it seemed to command the entire block. It was not as large as it first appeared—though it was large—and the homes about it were newer and more attractive. They had been built when people still cared about the things they lived in, before the era of glass and plastic and builders who pocketed the money that should have been used on foundation and structure. Some of the houses stood a story above the gothic nightmare, but somehow they had taken on a run-down, anemic look, as if the old grey house was in fact some sort of alien vampire that could impersonate a house by day, but late at night it would turn its head with a woodgrain creak, look out of its cold, rectangle eyes and suddenly stand to reveal thick peasant-girl legs and feet beneath its firm wooden skirt, and then it would start to stalk slowly and crazily down the street, the front door opening to reveal long, hollow, woodscrew teeth, and it would pick a house and latch onto it, fold back its rubbery front porch lips and burrow its many fangs into its brick or wood and suck out the architectural grace and all the love its builders had put into it. Then, as it turned to leave, bloated, satiated, the grass would die beneath its steps and it would creep and creak back down the street to find its place, and it would sigh deeply, contentedly, as it settled once more, and the energy and grace of the newer houses, the loved houses, would bubble inside its chest. Then it would sleep, digest, and wait.

"Let's go in," Clyde said.

The walk was made of thick white stones. They were cracked and weather-swollen. Some of them had partially tumbled out of the ground dragging behind a wad of dirt and grass roots that made them look like abscessed teeth that had fallen from some giant's rotten gums.

Avoiding the precarious stepping-stones, they mounted the porch, squeaked the screen and groaned the door open. Darkness seemed to crawl in there. They stepped inside.

"Hold it," Clyde said. He reached and hit the switch.

Darkness went away, but the light wasn't much. The overhead fixture was coated with dust and it gave the room a speckled look, like sunshine through camouflage netting.

There was a high staircase to their left and it wound up to a dangerous-looking landing where the railing dangled out of line and looked ready to fall. Beneath the stairs, and to the far right of the room, were many doors. Above, behind the landing, were others, a half dozen in a soldier row. Light slithered from beneath the crack of one.

"Well?" Clyde said.

"I sort of expect Dracula to come down those stairs any moment."

Clyde smiled. "He's down here with you, buddy. Right here."

"What nice teeth you have."

"Uh-huh, real nice. How about a tour?"

"Lead on."

"The basement first?"

"Whatever."

"All right, the basement then. Come on."

Above them, from the lighted room, came the sound of a girl giggling, then silence.

"Girls?" Brian asked.

"More about that later."

They crossed the room and went to a narrow doorway with a recessed door. Clyde opened it. It was dark and foul-smelling down there, the odor held you like an embrace.

Brian could see the first three stair steps clearly, three more in shadow, the hint of one more, then nothing.

"Come on," Clyde said.

Clyde didn't bother with the light, if there was one. He stepped on the first step and started down.

Brian watched as Clyde was consumed by darkness. Cold air washed up and over him. He followed.

At the border of light and shadow, Brian turned to look behind him. There was only a rectangle of light to see, and that light seemed almost reluctant to enter the basement, as if it too were fearful.

Brian turned back, stepped into the veil of darkness, felt his way carefully with toe and heel along the wooden path. He half-expected the stairs to withdraw with a jerk and pull him into some creature's mouth, like a toad tongue that had speared a stupid fly. It certainly smelled bad enough down there to be a creature's mouth.

Brian was standing beside Clyde now. He stopped, heard Clyde fumble in his leather jacket for something. There was a short, sharp sound like a single cricket-click, and a match jumped to life, waved its yellow-red head around, cast the youngsters' shadows on the wall, made them look like monstrous Siamese twins, or some kind of two-headed, four-armed beast.

Water was right at their feet. Another step and they would have been in it. A bead of sweat trickled from Brian's hair, ran down his nose and fell off. He realized that Clyde was testing him.

"Basements aren't worth shit around this part of the country," Clyde said, "except for a few things they're not intended for."

"Like what?" Brian asked calmly.

"You'll find out in plenty of time. Besides, how do I know I can trust you?"

That hurt Brian, but he didn't say anything. The first rule of being a Superman was to be above that sort of thing. You had to be strong, cool. Clyde would respect that sort of thing.

Clyde nodded at the water. "That's from last month's storm."

"Nice place if you raise catfish."

"Yeah."

The match went out. And somehow, Brian could sense Clyde's hand behind him, in a position to shove, considering it. Brian swallowed quietly, said very coolly, "Now what?"

After a long moment, Brian sensed Clyde's hand slip away, heard it crinkle into the pocket of his leather jacket. Clyde said, "Let's go back, unless you want to swim a little. Want to do that?"

"Didn't bring my trunks. Wouldn't want you to see my wee-wee."

Clyde laughed. "What's the matter, embarrassed at only having an inch?"

"Naw, was afraid you'd think it was some kind of big water snake and you'd try to cut it."

"How'd you know I had a knife?"

"Just figures."

"Maybe I like you."

"Big shit." But it was a big shit to Brian, and he was glad for the compliment, though he wasn't about to let on.

Clyde's jacket crinkled. Another match flared.

"Easy turning," Clyde said, "these stairs are narrow, maybe rotten."

Brian turned briskly, started up ahead of Clyde.

"Easy, I said."

Brian stopped. He was just at the edge of the light. He turned, smiled down. He didn't know if Clyde could see his smile in the match light or not, but he hoped he could feel it. He decided to try a little ploy of his own.

"Easy, hell," he said. "Didn't you bring me down here just to see if I'd panic? To see if those creaky stairs and that water and you putting a hand behind me would scare me?"

Clyde's match went out. Brian could no longer see him clearly. That made him nervous.

"Guess that was the idea," Clyde said from the darkness.

Another match smacked to life.

"Thought so."

Brian turned, started up, stepping firmly, but not hurriedly. The stairs rocked beneath his feet.

It felt good to step into the room's speckled light. Brian sighed softly, took a deep breath. It was a musty breath, but it beat the sour, rotten smell of the basement. He leaned against the wall, waited.

After what seemed like a long time, Clyde stepped out of the basement and closed the door. He turned to look at Brian, smiled.

(What nice teeth you have.)

"You'll do," Clyde said softly. "You'll do."

* * *

Now came the grand tour. Clyde led Brian through rooms stuffed with trash; full of the smell of piss, sweat, sex and dung; through empty rooms, cold and hollow as the inside of a petrified god's heart.

Rooms. So many rooms.

Finally the downstairs tour was finished and it was time to climb the stairs and find out what was waiting behind those doors, to look into the room filled with light.

They paused at the base of the stairs. Brian laid a hand on Clyde's shoulder.

"How in hell did you come by all this?" he asked.

Clyde smiled.

"Is it yours?" Brian asked.

"All mine," Clyde said. "Got it easy. Everything I do comes easy. One day I decided to move in and I did."

"How did you—"

"Hang on, listen: You see, this was once a fancy apartment house. Had a lot of old folks as customers, sort of an old fossil box. I needed a place to stay, was living on the streets then. I liked it here, but didn't have any money. So I found the caretaker. Place had a full-time one then. Guy with a crippled leg.

"I say to this gimp, I'm moving into the basement —wasn't full of water then—and if he don't like it, I'll push his face in for him. Told him if he called the cops I'd get him on account of I'm a juvenile and I've been in and out of kiddie court so many times I got a lunch card. Told him I knew about his kids, how pretty that little daughter of his was, how pretty I thought she'd look on the end of my dick. Told him I'd put her there and spin her around on it like a top. You see, I'd done my homework on the old fart, knew all about him, about his little girl and little boy.

"So, I scared him good. He didn't want any trouble and he let me and the cunt I was banging then move in."

A spark moved in Clyde's eyes. "About the cunt, just so you know I play hardball, she isn't around anymore. She and the brat she was going to have are taking an extended swimming lesson."

"You threw her in the bay?"

Clyde tossed his head at the basement.

"Ah," Brian said, and he felt an erection, a real blue-veiner. Something warm moved from the tips of his toes to the base of his skull, foamed inside his brain. It was as if his bladder had backed up and filled his body with urine. Old Clyde had actually killed somebody and had no remorse, was in fact proud. Brian liked that. It meant Clyde was as much of a Superman as he expected. And since Clyde admitted the murder to him, he knew he trusted him, considered him a comrade, a fellow Superman.

"What happened next?" Brian asked. It was all he could do not to lick his lips.

"Me and the cunt moved in. Couple guys I knew wanted to come too, bring their cunts along. I let them. Before long there's about a half dozen of us living in the goddamned basement. We got the caretaker to see we got fed, and he did it too on account of he was a weenie, and we kept reminding him how much we like little-girl pussy. I got to where I could describe what we wanted to do to her real good.

"Anyway, that went on for a while, then one day he doesn't show with the grub. Found out later that he'd packed up the dumpling wife, the two ankle-biters and split. So I say to the guys—by the way, don't ask no cunt nothing, they got opinions on everything and not a bit of it's worth stringy dogshit, unless you want to know the best way to put a Tampax in or what color goes well with blue . . . so, I say to the guys, this ain't no way to live, and we start a little storm trooper campaign. Scared piss out of some of the old folks, roughed up an old lady, nailed her dog to the door by its ears."

"Didn't the cops come around?"

"Yeah. They came and got us on complaints, told us to stay out. But what could they do? No one had seen us do a damn thing except those complaining, and it was just our word against theirs. They made us move out though.

"So, we went and had a little talk with the manager, made a few threats, got a room out of the deal and started paying rent. By this time we had the cunts hustling for us, bouncing tail on the streets and bringing in a few bucks. Once we start paying rent, what can they say? But we keep up the storm trooper campaign, just enough to keep it scary around here. Before long the manager quit and all the old folks hiked."

"What about the owner?"

"He came around. We paid the rent and he let us stay. He's a slumlord anyway. It was the old folks kept the place up. After they left, it got pretty trashy, and this guy wasn't going to put out a cent on the place. He was glad to take our money and run. We were paying him more than all the old codgers together. The pussy business was really raking in the coins. And besides, he don't want to make us mad, know what I mean?"

"Some setup."

"It's sweet all right. Like being a juvenile. The courts are all fucked up on that one. They don't know what to do with us, so they usually just say the hell with us. It's easier to let us go than to hassle with us. After you're eighteen life isn't worth living. That's when the rules start to apply to us too. Right now we're just misguided kids who'll straighten out in time."

"I understand."

"Good. Let's go upstairs. Got some people I want you to meet."

"Yeah?"

"A girl I want you to fuck."

"Yeah?"

"Yeah. Got this one cunt that's something else. Thirteen years old, a runaway or something. Picked her up off the street about a month ago. Totally wiped out in the brain department, not that a cunt's got much brain to begin with, but this one is a clean slate. But, man, does she have tits. They're big as footballs. She's as good a fuck as a grown woman."

"This going to cost me?"

"You kidding? You get what you want, no charge —money anyway."

"What's that mean?"

"I want your soul, not your money."

Brian grinned. "So who are you, the devil? Thought you were Dracula."

"I'm both of them."

"Do I have to sign something in blood?"

Clyde laughed hysterically. "Sure, that's a good one. Blood. Write something in fucking blood. I like you, Brian, I really do."

So Brian saw the dark rooms upstairs, and finally the one with the light and the people.

The room stank. There was a mattress on the floor and there was a nude girl on the mattress and there was a nude boy on the girl and the girl was not moving but the boy was moving a lot.

Another girl, with incredibly large breasts and large eyes, and a stocky-looking boy sat nude on the other side of the mattress and watched the boy on the girl. They lifted their heads as Clyde and Brian came in, and Brian could see that they were stoned to the max. The two smiled at them in unison, as if they had but one set of facial muscles between them.

The boy riding the girl grunted, once, real loud. After a moment he rolled off her smiling, his penis half-hard, dripping.

The girl on the mattress still did not move. She lay with her eyes closed and her arms by her sides.

"This is Loony Tunes," Clyde said, pointing to the boy who had just rolled off the girl. "This is Stone," he said, pointing to the stocky boy. "If he talks, I've never heard it." He did not introduce either girl. "This is all we got around here right now, cream of the crop."

The girl on the mattress still had not moved.

The one called Loony Tunes laughed once in a while, for no apparent reason.

Clyde said, "Go ahead and tend to your rat killing, me and Brian got plans." Then he snapped his fingers and pointed to the nude girl with the big breasts and the silly smile.

She stood up, wavering a bit. With ten pounds and something to truly smile about, she might have been pretty. She looked like she needed a bath.

Clyde held out his hand. She came around the mattress and took it. He put an arm around her waist.

The one called Stone crawled on top of the girl on the mattress.

She still did not move.

Brian could see now that her eyes were actually only half-closed and her eyeballs were partly visible. They looked as cool and expressionless as marbles.

Stone took hold of his sudden erection and put it in her.

She still did not move.

Stone began to grunt.

Loony Tunes laughed.

She still did not move.

"Come on," Clyde said to Brian, "the next room."

So they went out of there, the big-eyed girl sandwiched between them. Brian never saw the girl on the mattress again. And for that matter he never saw the dirty blond girl with the big brown eyes again after that night.

There was a small mattress in the closet in the next room, and Clyde, feeling his way around in the dark with experienced ease, pulled it out. Clyde said, "Keeping in practice for when I quit paying the light bill, learning to be a bat."

"I see," Brian said. The blonde leaned against him. She muttered something once, but it made no sense. She was so high on nose candy and cheap wine she didn't know where she was or who she was. She smelled like mildewed laundry.

After Clyde had tossed the mattress out on the floor, he took his clothes off, called them over. The blonde leaned on Brian all the way across the room.

When they were standing in front of Clyde, he said, "This is the big-tittied, thirteen-year-old I told you about. Looks older, don't she?" But he didn't wait for Brian to answer. He said loudly to the girl, "Come here."

She crawled on the mattress. Brian took his clothes off. They all lay down together. The mattress smelled of dirt, wine and sweat.

And that night Brian and Clyde had the thirteen-year-old and later, when Brian tried to think back on the moment, he would not be able to remember her face, only that she was blond, had massive breasts and dark eyes like pools of fresh-perked coffee; pools that went down and down and down into her head like wet tunnels to eternity.

She was so high they could have poked her with knives and she would not have felt it. She was just responding in automaton fashion. Clyde had it in her ass and Brian had it in her mouth, and they were pumping in unison, the smell of their exertion mingling with hers, filling the room.

The girl was slobbering and choking on Brian's penis and he was ramming it harder and harder into her mouth, and he could feel her teeth scraping his flesh, making his cock bleed, and it seemed to him that he was extending all the way down her throat, all the way through her, and that the head of his penis was touching Clyde's and Clyde's penis was like the finger of God giving life to the clay form of Adam, and that he was Adam, and he was receiving that spark from the Holy On High, and for the power and the glory he was grateful; made him think of the Frankenstein monster and how it must have felt when its creator threw the switch and drove the power of the storm through its body and above the roll of thunder and the crackling flash of lightning Dr. Frankenstein yelled at the top of his lungs, *"It's alive!"*

Then he and Clyde came in white-hot-atomic-blast unison and in Brian's mind it was the explosive ending of the old world and the Big Bang creation of the new . . .

Only the sound of panting now, the pleasant sensation of his orgasm draining into the blonde's mouth.

Clyde reached out and touched Brian's hand, squeezed his fingers, and Clyde's touch was as cold and clammy as the hand of death.

Clyde drove Brian home. Brian stole silently into the house and climbed the stairs. Once in his room he went to the window to look out. He could hear Clyde's '66 Chevy in the distance, and though it was a bright night and he could see real far, he could not see as far as Clyde had gone.

And later:
back at The House the girl Clyde and Brian had shared would start to wail and fight invisible harpies in her head, and Clyde would take her to the basement for a little swim. The body of the girl on the mattress would follow suit. Neither managed much swimming;

and there would be a series of unprecedented robberies that night all over the city;

and in a little quiet house near Galveston Bay, an Eagle Scout and honor student would kill his father and rape his mother;

and an on-duty policeman with a fine family and plenty of promotion to look forward to would pull over to the curb on a dark street and put his service revolver in his mouth and pull the trigger, coating the back windshield with brains, blood and clinging skull shrapnel;

and a nice meek housewife in a comfortable house by Sea Arama would take a carving knife to her husband's neck while he slept; would tell police later that it was because he said he didn't like the way she'd made roast that night, which was ridiculous since he'd liked it fixed exactly that same way the week before;

and in their tiny apartment, Monty and Becky Jones would frantically attempt to make love, but Becky wouldn't be able to find the mood and Monty wouldn't be able to find an erection. It seemed like an awful bad moment for the two of them, but this was because they had no idea how bad things were going to get.

All in all, it was a strange night in Galveston, Texas. A lot of dogs howled.

(2)
THE COUPLE

ONE

In early May, Becky and Montgomery Jones went to Galveston Beach. They took picnic supplies, a lusty appetite and a lot of nostalgia with them. Galveston Beach was where they had met years back. It had been May then too, and hot.

As Montgomery had admitted to Becky many times, the first thing he had noticed about her that day was the black string bikini she was wearing. He also admitted there had been quite a number of other bikinis he had taken notice of, but hers had quickly become his favorite when she'd walked by the towel where he was lying and he had watched her pass, enjoyed the shimmying twin moons of her ass split by the black eclipse of her bikini.

Because of this view, he had been forced to quit lying on his stomach, as things downstairs had rapidly become uncomfortable. But when he rolled on his side he found that his bathing suit was flying at half-mast, and had he rolled on his back, it would have looked as if he had erected a small pup tent for hamsters over his hips. So, he was forced to roll back on his stomach and ride the rail. From there he continued to watch the eclipsed moons until they pendulumed out of sight, were lost among other bodies, flashes of towels and rubber life rafts moving to and from the sea.

The bikinis that came after were merely wonderful or incredible, but nothing like the one that had fallen out of sight. Try as he might to focus on other nice hips and long, brown legs, those dual eclipsed moons his eyes had lost would not leave his mind.

Gathering up his suntan lotion, radio and towel —which he had draped across his shoulder in such a manner that it fell across his chest and erection— he made his stiff-legged way up the beach in search of that absolutely perfect bikini.

And lo and behold off the starboard bow, thar she blows, two soft, eclipsed moons were sinking slowly into the sea.

For the first time Montgomery began to think with the big head instead of the little head. Lifting his eyes beyond the natural homing point of sexual interest, he saw an absolutely gorgeous waist, bosom and face—for she had turned to climb toward land again, and as she came the water foamed mad-dog spittle around her legs and hips and she was as beautiful and mythical as that painting of Venus exploding from the sea. Oh yes, she was one fine-looking woman.

No. Fine wasn't the word. *Fine* meant: of superior quality or excellence. That had a near proper ring to it, but it just wasn't enough.

How about perfect? That was in the ballpark, but no closer to home plate than the home run fence— well, maybe, just maybe, as close as center-field, but not an inch closer.

Nope, the English language, the French language, the German language, etc., etc., were short on words for a woman like this.

She had . . . magic.

Then he thought: Maybe I'm just being starry-eyed. Up close she'll probably have the kind of teeth you could open a can of green beans with, or maybe a nice, bright bald spot on top of her head, or the kind of bad complexion that begins at the bone.

He decided he had to get closer, secretly fearing that up close his angel would turn out to be a moon howler.

Glancing down at his swim trunks he said to himself, "Lead on, Little Head."

As he went splashing out into the water he thought about the old trick of running into her and saying, "Excuse me, didn't see you wading there," but considering there were only three other people in the water in the immediate area, and they were about thirty feet away, the idea lacked charm.

No, he was going to be cool about this. Splash out to her like some sort of noble water god, make some cute Cary Grant remark and win her heart and soul immediately. He threw out his chest.

Oh God, the sunlight was hitting her hair and she was absolutely gorgeous; it looked as if there was a halo around her head, and

He fell.

No way to turn it into a dive and look casual. He had stepped right into a nice, slushy mass of sand, turned his ankle and fell.

One moment he's looking at the angel, next he's coughing salt and water and there's a sand burn on his knee and shin.

A wave washed over him, carried him back a yard, pulled his bathing suit down over his buttocks. He clutched at the suit, pulled it up as the water pushed him to shore.

He sat up. His towel was stuck to him and he had lost his suntan lotion and radio, but at least he had managed to pull his suit back up and, maybe, with more than a little luck, the angel hadn't gotten a flash of his lily-white ass sticking out of the waves. He hoped not. It was bad enough to be clumsy and lose your radio and suntan lotion (why hadn't he remembered he was carrying the goddamned radio and suntan lotion?), but to expose one's lily-white to an angel was unforgivable.

He looked around and saw her.

The angel was on the beach and she was looking at him. She had her hand over her mouth, was bent double and laughing; the worst kind of laugh, one of those sneaky kind you hold behind your hand so it won't explode like a bomb.

A wave came in, and his suntan lotion floated up. Neat. The radio cost $19.95 and what floats up? The $2.98 suntan lotion.

He clutched the lotion, looked at the angel. He could see teeth on either side of her hand now, and he was surprised to discover that a person really could grin from ear to ear.

This was beginning to make him a little angry.

He stood up, moved his foot about in the sand, hoping to find the radio. No luck.

"Pardon me," he said, looking at the angel, who looked close to hyperventilation.

"Wha . . . ?" she tried.

He slapped wet sand from his legs and bathing suit, waded to shore. The towel clung to him like a sash. The suntan lotion was clutched in his hand like a blunt instrument—well, it was a thought.

"Pardon me," he repeated. "Someone tell you a good joke?"

"Unnuh," she said, and it just got out from

behind her fingers before she exploded into hysterical laughter.

"No, huh?"

". . . n . . . no." Didn't she know it was impolite to drop to one knee laughing?

"No?"

She took a deep breath, stood. "Just *saw* a good joke."

"Nice."

"Are you always so clumsy?"

"Mostly just when I'm trying to impress good-looking women."

"I'm impressed."

"I can see that. Works every time."

"I see. You see an attractive woman and you fall down?"

"It's a killer, isn't it?"

"Have you thought about using leg braces when you go girl watching?"

"The braces rust in this salt air."

"So you don't think leg braces would solve the problem?"

"Speaking of legs, that's certainly a nice pair you use to carry you around."

"Oh, so it's my legs you noticed, nothing else?"

"How can I tell you I like your brain when we haven't even met. All I know is what I see, and I like that. But maybe I'll find out you're not too bright and that you have disgusting bathroom habits."

"Oh, I don't think you'll have to worry about finding out much."

"Uh-oh, hurt your feelings. I'm just saying I'd like to find out if you're . . . smart."

"I'm smart enough to see where this is going. And that's what I'm doing, going."

"Guess I said something wrong, showed my ass?"

"Yes, you have—in more ways than one. And it's very white and not very good-looking. I think I saw pimples on it."

"You did see . . . ?"

"It was hard to miss."

"Look, I was just trying to impress you—"

"You have, all right. Go fish for your radio."

"Look, look, don't walk off. I fell. You saw my ass, and then I tried to impress you with my suave recovery, and I was doing okay until I had a male chauvinistic relapse, the stuff about your legs. But I mean . . . you wouldn't wear that if you didn't want men to look . . . shit."

"Open mouth, insert other foot."

She bent to pick up a large blue towel from the beach.

"That yours?" he said, and immediately regretted it.

"No, I steal these when I come across them. Sew them together and they make fabulous bedspreads, great Christmas gifts."

"I don't seem to be doing so good."

"No, you don't."

She began walking away.

"Hey," he said, bounding after her, "you can't walk away like that."

"Oh no, here I go."

"You can't do that. Don't walk away like that."

She turned a furious face on him, slung the towel over her shoulder. "How about like this?" And she began taking long, ridiculous strides.

Montgomery couldn't help himself. He began to laugh.

She went a few more steps, turned with her hands on her hips, then she laughed. "Hey, you," she said, "walk this way," and she started off across the sand taking those ridiculous strides, and Montgomery followed mocking her walk, and pretty soon they were side by side laughing.

They stopped walking.

"Look," Montgomery said, "I'm sorry. Let's start over."

"All right."

"My, but don't I know you from somewhere?"

"No. My name is Becky Shiner."

"And my name is Montgomery Jones."

"Have you considered changing it?"

"Often."

"That's one of the worst names I've ever heard."

"Not quite. The middle name is Buford."

"You're pulling my leg?"

"I wish I were . . . shit."

"Maybe later."

"Yeah?"

"Down boy."

"Sorry."

"Montgomery Buford Jones. Hummm. God, that's awful! Are you a second or a junior?"

"Actually, I'm a junior, but forget that."

"Montgomery Buford Jones, Jr—"

"You're not forgetting."

"—will you buy me a hot dog?"

"You kidding? I'll rob the goddamned stand if you want me to."

"I'll settle for you buying me a hot dog. We'll knock over a filling station later."

Not long after, Montgomery got money from the glove box of his car. They bought and ate hot dogs, they walked along the beach holding hands, and talked until the sun pooped out and the moon

checked in. They discussed everything. Politics.
Religion. He told her about his part-time job and
she told him about her part-time job, and he told
her how he was finishing up college in a year at the
University of Houston, and she told him she was
doing the same and wasn't it amazing that they had
never met, and he said, I'll say, and wouldn't it be
nice if we took some classes together, and she said
yeah, and then he told her things about himself,
and how he had tried out for sports in high school
and had fallen down a lot, and she told him how
she had been on the track and swim team and had
been quite good at both, and for him not to take
this personal, but it didn't look as if he had become
any more athletic than before, considering his
dramatic entrance into the water today, and he
laughed at that, and they continued to talk about
anything and everything until it was very, very late.

They went to his apartment in Houston that first
night.

on me.
on me, Monty.
"Monty. Oh, Monty."
"What?"
"Remember me, your wife? The girl lying next to
you on the beach towel? Will you put some suntan
lotion on me?"
"Shit, I'm sorry. I was daydreaming."
"About long, brown legs, I bet."
"Yep."
"Well, you shit."
"About yours."
"I bet."
"I was."

"Don't snow me, Mr. Montgomery Buford Jones, Jr."

He put an arm around her. "I was thinking about how we met."

She wrinkled her nose at him. "Oh, and how was that? I don't seem to remember. Seems you've always been with me. Like a birth defect."

"There's always plastic surgery."

"You'd just leave a scar."

"I hope so."

"Were you really thinking about my legs?"

"Yep."

"Do you ever think about other women's legs?"

"God forbid."

"Monty, come on."

"Sometimes?"

"Do you ever think about more than the legs?"

"Sometimes."

"Shithead."

"Sometimes."

"Well, did you know I masturbate to Tom Jones albums when I'm home alone? I just think about that gyrating hunk of man and blammo, double, triple orgasms."

"Sounds nice."

"It is."

"Right there in the living room, huh?"

"Yep, on the couch."

"I see, and I thought that smell was cat piss on the cushions."

"You shithead."

"Sometimes."

"All the time. Here, put this lotion on me."

"How's that?"

"Ummmm."

"Becky?"

"Yes."

"What did you ever do with that black string bikini?"

"It's at home."

"Can you still fit into it?"

"I ought to slap your face, Montgomery Buford Jones, Jr. You know I can. I've gained a pound or two, but nothing that would spill out. Or haven't you noticed?"

"I notice."

"I bet you don't even look at me anymore."

"I look. Why didn't you wear it today?"

"I haven't worn it in years."

"Why?"

"I'm old-fashioned."

"You weren't old-fashioned when I saw you in it—what there was of it."

"I was shopping then."

"My goodness, that doesn't sound very liberated."

"Truth."

"So why don't you wear it now?"

"Like I said, I was shopping. I've got you nabbed now, for what that's worth. Besides, doesn't this one look nice enough?"

"There's too much of it."

"I believe that was a male chauvinistic remark, Mr. Montgomery Buford Jones, Jr."

"Definitely."

"What will all your liberal pals say?"

"May I look at your wife's ass, probably."

"Monty."

"I'm not kidding. Have you seen their wives? Yetch, right out of the pound. Besides, what am I, a eunuch? I like the way you look in that thing."

"Okay, I'll wear it for you next time we come to the beach."

"No way."

"You're impossible."

"You could wear it tonight, at home. That way I'd get to see you in it and Galveston Beach wouldn't have to have its sand dried out."

"What?"

"From all the saliva these male wolves would drip on it when they saw you in that thing."

"Would you like a poke in the nose?"

"How about a kiss?"

"Close enough."

"Lower."

"My God, Monty."

"Not that low."

"We're saving that for home too?"

"You bet, sweetheart. Now kiss me. On the lips."

"Not bad. Now will you finish with rubbing the suntan oil on already?"

He began rubbing the oil on her back, copping a bit of breast feel around the sides.

"Stop that, Monty."

"Okay."

"Don't you dare . . . Monty?"

"Hummmm?"

"We'll never let anything come between us, will we?"

"What could come between us?"

"We never will, will we?"

"Hey, why so serious?"

"Just answer me."

"Come on, what could come between us?"

"Promise me nothing will. No matter how bad things might get, promise nothing will."

"Things aren't going to get bad. Another couple

of years we're going to be chasing little rug rats around until they're grown and we'll probably die in bed at one hundred and six while performing sixty-nine."

"Seriously, promise." She rolled over on her side to look up at him.

"Okay, baby. I promise. Nothing, no matter how crazy, how bad, how terrible, will ever come between us. And you can tuck that in a sock and store it."

TWO

Later that day, back at their apartment, Becky wore the bikini for Montgomery. But only for a little while. They made long, slow, sweet love through the rest of the afternoon and there were no problems. Becky thought it was the best ever.

So by the grace of the sun and the sea and their memories, they had renewed their love and the summer fled on, dragging behind it the good times, running wild, not knowing where the future led.

And the Dark Side Clock ticked on.

(3)
THE CAULDRON BUBBLES

ONE

From the May 22 edition of the *Galveston News*, page 1.

RAPIST RIPPER STRIKES AGAIN

The fifth in a series of brutal, unsolved attacks on women occurred last night at 304 Strand Street. The latest victim was 26-year-old Lena Carruthers. Police say the method of attack, rape and murder by slicing the victim's throat, fits the pattern established by the last four attacks, the first of which occurred late October. New evidence suggests that the Rapist Ripper, as he is now called, may in fact be more than one man. Police . . .

TWO

From the journal of Brian Blackwood, entry date, May 23.

Last night I awoke and didn't know where I was. Just woke up and couldn't put it together, and when finally I get it figured that I'm staying over at The House, I roll over and there's Clyde standing by my bed without a stitch on. He's just looking down at me, and I say, "Hey, what's up?" and he doesn't say a goddamned word. Just stands there by the bed in the dark, looking, not doing anything, just looking at me, his eyes all crazy and zombielike, and then I get it figured. Clyde's a sleepwalker.

I didn't know what to do. Heard that you don't wake a sleepwalker on account of he might die. I don't really believe that shit, but I didn't want to take any chances, yet didn't know what else to do. Finally I think, get off the superstitious crap, so I say his name. He didn't do anything the first time, but when I called it again, a little louder, he says, "It's so lovely, the blood and all. Just damn fine."

. And then I realize he's talking about what we did last night, and that he's still not awake. But by then he turns and walks out of there leaving me feeling like we just shot a scene from one of those second-feature, drive-in, Z brand movies.

Gave me the goddamned creeps, I'll tell you, Mr.

Journal, but that's between you and me. I kind of liked it too. I mean, that's the thing with Clyde. He's always doing the unexpected. Nothing normal happens around the guy and the unusual is starting to happen around me too.

Neat.

THREE

This headline from the June 12 edition of the *Galveston News:*

RIPPER KILLS AND RAPES SIXTH

FOUR

June 15

"I've been watching her."

"She look good?"

"Oh yeah. You know her. She's from the high school."

"Yeah?"

"A teacher, Mrs. Jones. Teaches some sociology and history."

"Oh yeah, I know her, all right. What a piece. But she knows us."

"So? You, me, Stone and Loony are the Rapist Ripper, remember? There's the ripper part too."

"Yeah, right. Of course. When?"

"Tonight."

"We're doing them kind of close, aren't we, Clyde?"

"You trying to work with the full moon or something?"

"No, just worried about the cops some."

"Say, Brian, if we do them months apart and they can't catch us, what makes you think they can catch us any better if we do one a day?"

"Yeah, guess you're right."

"You know I'm right. Tonight then?"

"Right. Tonight."

FIVE

June 15, 7:45 P.M.

"Did you palm that bishop?"

"Shit! Caught me."

"Tsk, tsk. If you're going to cheat at chess, Eva, you're going to have to do better than that."

Eva held up her left hand. "Does that mean I

have to give back the pawn too, Beck?" She opened her hand. A white, plastic pawn lay in the center, with the bishop.

"You shit. How long ago did you do that?"

"Back when you took my rook. It just didn't seem right, you mopping up the board and me not getting anything."

"If you'd quit trying to play the pieces like checkers, you'd do better."

"Then let's play checkers."

"No way. You're too good at that, and I don't palm checkers half as well as you do chess pieces, bad as that is."

"Unfair, you won't play my game."

"My apartment, nah, nah, nah, nah, nah."

"Still unfair."

"Put the bishop and the pawn back, Eva. Not there—where they belong."

"Happy?"

"Uh-huh, checkmate."

"Good, I'm glad to have it over with."

"Another drink?"

"No, I'm driving."

"Yeah, couple of teas and you go all to pieces."

"Not kidding, Beck, caffeine eats me up. Tears apart what brain I got left."

"Okay, I'll have another."

"Oh, what the hell, I'll live dangerously. Make it two sugars and don't hold back on the lemon."

Becky rose, went to the little kitchenette.

"You know, Beck, it's sort of fun to get away from the guys for a while. I love my old jackass, but it sure is good not to hear him bray for a bit."

"It's fine unless you have to stay by yourself for a couple days. Did you say two sugars?"

"Right, two. True enough. I'm going home to my

jackass, but yours won't be around. Say, you want me to call Dean and tell him I'm staying over?"

"No, you've got to go to work in the morning. Me, I'm free as a bird."

"Lucky you."

"Yeah, lucky me. We took the summer off just like we could afford it. I probably should have taught summer classes, Monty too. Our bank account is taking the summer off too."

"Well, Monty's getting paid for that thing he went to in Houston, isn't he? Whatever the hell it is."

"A conference for sociologists. Bunch of speakers on juvenile problems, stuff like that."

"Why didn't you go? Your field too."

"Didn't want to. You know, Eva, I've got a confession. I want to quit teaching."

"Be a housewife?"

"Not hardly."

"Good, you haven't got enough practice. This place looks horrible."

"Wrong. The panty hose on the shower rod is avant-garde decoration. You're just not with it."

"That the case? Hey, are you having to grow and cure the tea leaves over there?"

"No, but I am boiling them. It's the way tea's made. Would you like a couple tea bags to suck on while you wait?"

"No, but the part about the bags reminds me of an incredibly filthy joke, but I'll refrain."

"Thank God for small favors."

"You still haven't told me why you want to quit teaching. I was trying to be discreet and not too nosey because I thought you were going to work it into the conversation."

"I don't know . . . just don't enjoy it that much

lately. Seems like to me the kids just don't give a damn. And there are some that are just creeps; they scare me. When I was a kid the whole idea of scaring a teacher would never have entered my mind, wouldn't have believed it possible. To me teachers were gods of a sort, those who give thee information. But now . . . sometimes just looking at my students, at their eyes, gives me the creeps."

"Makes you wonder if all the nasty stuff in our food these days is causing mothers to give birth to a race of evil mutants, huh? Makes me think of this movie I saw once where a whole village of children were somehow affected in the womb, and they all grew up with super powers and stuff, scared the shit out of the adults."

"Well, they don't have to have weird powers to frighten me, they do quite nicely without them—some of them. Lot of good kids too. I'm just hard-pressed to think of one at the moment."

Eva laughed.

"But it's not just that," Becky continued. "I just need a change. Nothing new is happening in my life. I'm not unhappy. Monty and I are fine. I'm just bored with what I do is all."

"I sort of know what you mean . . . We've come a long way from when we were going to save the world, haven't we, Beck?"

"You said lemon?"

"Yes."

"Yeah, we've come a long way. Wish I could be as idealistic as I used to be, as Monty is. He truly believes in his fellowman, that man is basically good, and that if you could just get enough people to listen they'd try to be good and kind to one another, and the world would change and be a wonderful place to live."

"Sounds like a Disney movie. Do you believe that?"

"No."

"Good. It's a crock of shit."

Becky brought the tea over, sat back down. "He was telling me that if there was a shortage of food, a sudden thing where the grocery stores were emptying out, that there would be a bit of rioting, some chaos, but that most would reason and try to hold together, and they'd make an effort to see that everyone was fed and taken care of. So on and so on."

"Now we're talking Bambi picture. Maybe at one time it might have been that way, I mean to some degree. But man is a meat-eating beast, and I think if you tried to stand in front of a bunch of hungry, crazed folks you'd wind up with shoe prints on your head, and maybe end up half-eaten."

"So do I. I'm even beginning to think those Survivalists aren't that crazy. I mean, I used to look at them like they were kooks. But I'm not so sure anymore."

"Monty is naive . . . But he is a good-looking rascal. How'd you end up with him and I ended up with old, ugly Dean?"

"He's not ugly."

"Beck."

"Okay, he's kind of ugly, but he's sweet."

Eva laughed.

"And you ended up with him because you loved him."

"Yeah, I guess. And you know what? I still do. You know what else?"

"What?"

"If we can be that crazy about our husbands after all these years, guess that goes to show there's some love in the human race. No Bambi picture here, but maybe that proves something."

"Know what you mean." Becky lifted her tea glass. "To our husbands and our marriages, and the betterment of the world."

They toasted, drank.

A hot June wind gnawed at the windows and rattled the front door.

SIX

9:20 P.M.

The black '66 Chevy rolled through the night, Clyde at the wheel, Brian by his side, Loony Tunes and Stone in the back, passing a bottle wrapped tight in a paper sack between them.

"Are we ready?" Clyde asked.

"Yes," Brian and Loony said in unison. Stone nodded.

"Good," Clyde said.

SEVEN

"Guess I better be going, Beck."

"It's been fun."

"Look, you want me to call Dean and see about staying over? I don't like the idea of you staying here alone."

"No, that's all right."

"I don't mind."

"I know, but it's okay."

"You're sure?"

"I'm sure. I'm going to watch the late movie, give me something to do."

"One of those Japanese monster flicks, no doubt?"

"*No Way to Treat a Lady*, something like that."

"All right, but don't be surprised if I come back knocking on your door. You look like a forlorn pup."

"Really, I'm all right. No need to worry. I'm going to listen to Ray Charles a bit, then when the movie comes on I'll watch that. Might even blow my diet and make some popcorn."

"That's incentive enough for me to stay."

"I'm all right, really, Eva. I'm a big girl now."

"Okay, don't share your old popcorn . . . It's just

with the things that have been happening, the Rapist Ripper stuff . . ."

"Hush, hush, I don't need that on my mind."

"Sorry."

Becky walked Eva to the door.

"Listen, Beck. You get lonely, call me. Anytime of the night, got me?"

"Got you."

"Promise?"

"For Christsakes, I promise."

"Bye, Beck, and good night . . . and don't be surprised if I get as far as the parking lot and decide to come back and make you let me stay."

Becky smiled, opened the door. A hot wind hit the air-conditioned apartment. The contrast made Becky's stomach turn.

"Christ," Eva said, "you'd think we were having one of those California devil winds, what are they called? Santa Anas?"

"Be careful."

"I will. Later."

Becky watched Eva walk along the outside landing and start down the steps. Just before she disappeared down the stairs she smiled back at Becky and waved.

Becky returned the smile and the wave, closed the door.

EIGHT

The black '66 killed its lights, coasted onto the apartment lot like a metal shark on a concrete sea.

"This is the place?" Loony said.

"No," Clyde said. "I just thought I'd stop here for the hell of it."

"Okay," Loony said, "I wasn't thinking."

"You're never thinking," Brian said.

"I didn't mean nothing by it, I was just talking."

"Shut the fuck up, Loony," Clyde said.

Clyde cut the engine, and it was as if a million locusts had suddenly stopped beating their wings; it was abnormally silent. They sat in the darkness, the hot wind blowing through the open windows. They passed the bottle around. No one spoke.

A woman swirled out of the apartment Clyde was watching, came down the stairs walking fast, entered the shadows, was swallowed by them then regurgitated into one of the alternating lights along the railing. Darkness. Light. Darkness. Light. Every few seconds her blue and white polka-dot dress shone in the light like the wings of a great moth, then she would be a form in darkness, the dress suddenly dark as bat wings.

"How about her?" Loony asked.

"No. I have someone else in mind."

The woman moved to a small car, opened the door. The interior light glowed, the moth wings shone momentarily as she swung inside, then the door slammed and there was darkness followed by the hum of the engine. Headlights came on, and then she was gone.

"What's it matter who?" Loony said. "She looked good enough for me. All pink on the inside, ain't it?"

"I got my reasons," Clyde said. "I like the way the teacher looks. One time she was nice to me, and I haven't forgot it."

Loony laughed. "She was nice to you so you're going to rape her and cut her throat. Boy, I like that."

Clyde turned around in his seat where he could look at Loony. Loony's face became as expressionless as Stone's. "I'm going to tell you this once, dung ball, just once. I got the say-so here. What I say, we do, and if I'm not around to say it Brian says it. That simple. You got it, dung ball?"

"Yeah, yeah, I got it."

"Good. You keep the thought and hold it like a baby holding a teddy bear. Don't let it go, Loony, 'cause so help me, I'm going to give this car a red paint job—with your blood.

"I said I got you. I got you."

"Good." Clyde turned around.

A hot wind blew through the car and curled the hairs on their necks and heads. Out somewhere in the sticky night void, a car honked and a dozen motors gunned away from a red light.

"We're going to do it this way," Clyde said. "Me and Stone are going up this time, and you two are going to watch."

"Hey, it's my turn," Loony said. "Stone went up last time."

"Stone doesn't act like a dung ball," Clyde said. "Now shut up and take the shotgun. I want you by the stairs. Hear me?"

"I hear," Loony said. He bent, picked a pump 12-gauge from the floorboard, laid it in his lap. The barrel struck Stone in the balls, and without saying a word, Stone pushed it aside with the palm of his hand.

Loony turned to look at Stone, saw that he was frowning. He moved the shotgun so that it was pointing at the roof of the car. Loony felt exasperated and mad. He couldn't do anything right tonight.

"You guys stay in the car a minute," Clyde said. "Got to talk some private shit to my main man here."

Clyde opened the door and got out. Brian followed suit. They walked around in front of the car.

"Main man," Loony hissed under his breath. "Goddamn butthole buddies."

Out in front of the car Clyde said, "I'm not slighting you."

"I know. We're taking turns."

"Not just that. I want a good man downstairs. Loony's too full of glue tonight. I need some brains down here. Stone does as he's told, but I need more than that."

"No sweat. Fuck her for me."

"I will, and I'll cut half her throat for you."

"That part about her being nice to you. That true?"

"Yeah. Long time ago. She kept some big kid off me in a school fight. I could have licked him though. But I've wanted her ass ever since."

"Dreams come true."

Clyde took a switchblade from his pocket, flicked it open. "Guess they do."

NINE

Raymond Caldwell was constipated and the poodle needed to shit.

Typical.

The wife didn't give a damn that the crap had dried up inside of him like a goddamned concrete pillar, but she was next to hysterically urgent when she thought the pink-toed poodle with the curly, shampooed hair might be a few seconds late with its bowel movement, and of course he was the one that had won the honor of taking MeMe out for a dump.

Swell, he had a boulder hung in his ass, and prissy mutt needed to drop a load. And right when it was time for the wrestling matches, and he's waited all week for them too. Tonight was the night the Raider was going to give that kraut bastard Eric Von Stropper the old what for, twist his ugly head right off of his ugly shoulders. Probably be blood and the sound of cracking bones all over the place—and guess who needed to shit?

Guess where he'd be when the blood started flying?

Downstairs watching a poodle lose a noodle.

Good old MeMe, that dog was a hundred years old. Why didn't she die? The goddamned dog was going to outlive him. Here he was seventy and next year his chair would be empty and the goddamned dog would be laying there watching wrestling.

"Christ, Selma, can't you take the dog out to shit? It's almost time for the matches."

"Ray, such language. MeMe can't go to the toilet like we can."

"So who's going to the toilet these days. I feel like I got a cork in my ass."

"Ray, I will not stand for that sort of language in this house."

"This isn't a house, it's a goddamned apartment."

"Ray."

"Don't give me that Ray crap. Every time you get that tone in your voice it means I'm not going to get any. Big deal. Ten years ago it was still a big deal. Not now. Hold out if you want. I couldn't get this old salami up with a crane."

"Ray, you take MeMe out this instant."

"It's embarrassing for a grown man to stand around and watch a goddamned poodle leave its calling card. I feel like everybody's getting snapshots. If we're going to have a dog, why don't we get something like a shepherd, something with some dignity. Not this rat with a hairdo."

"I can be very hard to live with, Ray."

"Believe me, I know it. You're hard to live with now. Look here, for Christsake, the matches are coming on."

She looked at the television. "They still have to call each other names for a while and there's always a couple of commercials first . . . You know I can't go out there. A woman alone—"

"Yeah, yeah, all the guys are just hanging out of windows to get a look at you."

"I wasn't so bad in my time."

"So the dinosaurs are dead now, Selma."

"And you're a year older than me."

"Oh, for crying out loud. Give me the god-damned leash and let me get it over with."

"And don't forget the poopy scooper."

"I'm not scooping up no fresh dogshit."

"You can't leave it just lying around. Someone will step in it. You got to take it to the dumpster."

"Oh hell, give me the goddamned poopy scooper."

TEN

9:47 P.M.

Becky put on a Ray Charles album, moved the needle to her favorite, "Born to Lose."

There was a knock on the door.

She smiled. That darn Eva, she thought. She went to the door, opened it with a jerk.

It wasn't Eva.

9:50 P.M.

MeMe was really hunkered, and Raymond was glad to see the little pooch was having a hard time. Maybe the goddamned dog would strain itself to death. Serve the little bitch right. He nearly died twice a day, and the hemorrhoids, Christsake, like footballs.

Someone screamed—shortly, as if it had been quickly muffled.

Raymond turned. It came from across the way, from the upper deck of apartments.

He jerked on MeMe's leash, began moving toward the stairs. Then common sense got the better of him. Now, just a minute, he thought. Probably it was nothing except some husband with a big poker putting it to . . .

Another scream, this one muffled like the first, as if the voice had crept out from behind a hand, and had just as quickly been recaptured.

Definitely upstairs, Raymond thought. He moved off the grassy section of the lot and into the shadows, making his way toward the stairs. He went around the dumpster and saw a form standing twenty feet away, one foot on the bottom stair step. The man was turned so that his back was to him, and Raymond could see that he held a rifle or shotgun.

Raymond let go of the leash and gripping the poopy scooper like a baseball bat, stepped briskly toward the sentry, his heart beating with the rhythmic thumping of a boxer's speed bag.

And then, just as he was even with the steps and there was only the metal stairs and their open gaps separating him from the man with the gun, the guy turned.

It was a kid, and the kid's face jumped into a surprised expression and the shotgun—for he could see now that it was a shotgun—raised, and the kid was starting to point it at him through the stair gaps.

Raymond slammed the scooper against the side

of the barrel and the gun went hard right and there was an explosion, and he thought, am I dead?

A second later he determined he was not even hit, and he reached the barrel with one hand, and with a quick wrenching action, pulled it out of the kid's grasp and through the steps.

The kid yelled something at him and came around the stairs, teeth bared in a mad-dog smile.

Raymond dropped the shotgun and laid the scooper, with a nice, wind-whistling, both-handed swing, upside the kid's head.

The kid went down.

Raymond swung the scooper again and when he hit the kid's skull, blood jumped up like a dark liquid shadow and fell to the cement lot.

The kid fell forward on his face. Out.

MeMe ran up and began chewing on the kid's leg.

Raymond picked up the shotgun and started upstairs, hoping to locate the source of the scream. Fishy things going on, an ocean full of fishy things.

At the top of the stairs he stopped and looked down. The kid was still out. The poopy scooper lay where he had dropped it in place of the shotgun, and MeMe was chewing on the kid's shoe, jerking and growling savagely. Well, he thought, maybe the little shit isn't so bad after all. "Good dog," he said.

He pumped a round into the 12-gauge.

Brian had been standing guard at the car, watching the street entrance. Loony's job was to watch the lot and the stairs. But the sound of the shotgun blast had caused him to turn.

In the shadows, some distance away, he saw two people struggling. He recognized one shape as Loony, and he saw that shape grab its head and go

down. The other figure had something in his hand
and he was hitting Loony with it, and in a moment
he realized that the man now had the shotgun and
was going upstairs. A little dog was chewing on
Loony's leg.

"Damn," Brian said softly.

He jumped in the Chevy, gunned it to life. Most
likely Clyde and Stone had heard the shotgun
blast, but if not . . .

He hit down three hard times on the horn.

Raymond, now moving across the landing, listening and watching for who knows what, heard the
horn too. He glanced toward the lot, saw lights
coming fast toward the apartment building.

Then, to his right, he heard another sound and
he whirled.

The door directly to his right burst open and two
bodies slammed into him and he fell back against
the railing, the shotgun went out of his hands and
over and he almost followed.

Fists slammed his head and he slid down to the
landing with his back against the rail. All he could
see were legs. He could hear music—that black
guy, Ray Charles—and between the legs he could
see a woman lying on the floor, naked, gagged, her
arms stretched out and tied to furniture.

Then the legs he was looking through began to
move, kicking at him. Hurting him.

And he remembered Raider and his famous
scissor move and how he had once put it on Leroy
Jerowsky, and how he had brought Jerowsky down
so hard he'd cracked his head open.

Another kick in the chest and he rolled and
slapped out with his old legs and caught one pair of
the kicking legs above the knees and twisted. The
boy went forward and hit the railing with his

forehead and it made a nice pleasant sound, sort of like someone tossing up a cantaloupe and swatting it with a two-by-four. The kid fell down beside him.

He tried to wiggle his legs from around him and get up, but the other kid kicked him in the head, hard.

Raymond started crawling, but the legs followed him, kicking.

He passed out for a moment.

The legs went away.

There was some yelling below. He heard MeMe yelp once. Something sharp went into his throat, twisted, and he felt wet warmth on his face and chest, and his last thought was that he was going to miss the goddamned wrestling matches, and this one was for the belt too.

He rolled over on top of the unconscious boy.

ELEVEN

Black '66 Chevy moving fast. Three inside. Brian driving, Loony, holding his head, blood oozing through his fingers, the dead poodle on the floorboard, appearing to be red-furred, and Stone in the back, his head hung down.

"You stupid motherfuckers," Brian said. "You stupid motherfuckers. Throw that goddamned dog out!"

"I'm going to stuff the motherfucker," Loony

said. "I'm going to stuff the little motherfucker and use him to kick like a fucking football."

"Throw that goddamned dog out, you moron!"

"Cocksucker nearly chewed my leg off—"

"Throw that fucking dog out, or so help me the devil, I'm going to throw you out."

Loony took the bloody dog by the scruff of the neck and tossed it. Pearls of its blood splattered the side of the car, blew in on Stone, decorated his face like a strawberry explosion. He didn't move, still sat with his head half-hung.

"Loony," Brian said, "you ignorant shit. You stupid motherfucker. And you, Stone, you went off and left Clyde. What's with you, man?"

Stone shook his head violently. There were tears in his eyes. He slapped his hand beaver-tail-like on the seat beside him. He made a sound somewhere between a cry and a moan.

Brian ran a red light, took a right down a side street, drove fast.

Black '66 blending with the night. Gone.

(4)
POSSESSION

ONE

And so the summer moved on.

Clyde named no cohorts, and the three who had been with him breathed deep sighs, and Brian told the other two thoughtfully: "Well, I'm not surprised. He's a Superman."

And not long after that the Superman hung himself from his cell bars, and Brian, on many a night, had to ask himself why.

The House was abandoned (later the slumlord would be forced to renovate, and in the water-filled basement bodies would be found and the papers would be full of it), and Stone and Loony went their way for a while, came to see Brian at his house on dark nights after the street had put itself to bed.

The three played it cool and silent.

The newspaper, the television and the radio news eventually gave up on the novelty of the Rapist Ripper; lost interest in the fact that the human components that had made up the whole were free somewhere.

No more Rapist Ripper attacks occurred. Galveston sighed and became complacent.

And summer became fall.

And Brian, one night in mid-October, slept in his bed and felt the first tentative wigglings of a tentacle in his brain.

He dreamed of this long narrow alley all wrapped in darkness, and up this alley, slow-walking with a plopping sound, came a shape, and somehow Brian knew the shape was a demon-god and the demon-god was called the God of the Razor.

Down the alley of his mind came the demon-god, and Brian was afraid. He tried to wake up, but no soap. He tried to will it away, but no soap.

On came the demon-god, making a horrible plopping sound as he walked.

Very close now. And clearly visible as he folded out of darkness.

The God of the Razor was tall, black—not Negro, but *black*—with shattered starlight eyes and teeth like thirty-two polished, silver stickpins. He had on a top hat that winked of chrome razor blades molded into a bright hatband. His coat (and Brian was not sure how he knew this, but he did) was the skinned flesh of an ancient Aztec warrior and his pants were the same. Raw, bloody fingers stuck out of his pants pockets like stashed after-dinner treats, and the Dark Side Clock (another thing he knew, but did not understand), which was an enormous pocket watch, dangled from a strand of gut attached to the God's vest pocket—a pocket that was once the fleshy slit that housed an eye. The shoes he wore (another unexplained knowledge) were the ragged heads of guillotined Frenchmen from a long-dead revolution. The God's cloven feet fit nicely into those dead mouths and when he walked the heads thudded like medicine balls being slow-bounced along a hardwood floor.

And the God's fingernails were not nails at all, but razor blades. He kept rubbing them together as he walked, making them click and pop up sparks.

Then he was very close and out of nowhere he popped out a chair made of human leg bones with a seat of woven ribs, hunks of flesh, hanks of hair, and he seated himself, crossed his legs, dangled one ragged head shoe, produced from thin air a ventriloquist dummy and put it on his knee. The dummy wore tennis shoes, jeans, a black tee-shirt and a leather jacket with zippers, and the face was the wood-carved, ridiculously red-cheeked face of Clyde.

The God shoved his hand into the back of the Clyde dummy, pushed it forward and placed it on his knee. The dummy opened its mouth, "Been jacking around long enough, haven't you?"

Brian tried to speak, but couldn't. He couldn't determine where he was located in the dream.

"Time to get cracking," the dummy said. "We got work to do. That bitch of a teacher didn't get what she should have gotten, and it's up to you to see that she does."

Brian still couldn't speak. He did not feel as if he were dreaming. He was frightened.

"You know who my pal here is, don't you?" said the dummy.

"The God of the Razor," Brian said, suddenly finding his voice.

"Right. A big cigar. Those that have the call know him when they see him. You might say I'm his puppet, have been all along. And you are my puppet. I'm going to be living inside your head.

Moving in the furniture tonight . . . and you're going to pay the rent and utilities. Got me?"

"I think so."

"Sure you do. Now, I want to get those shitheads together, Loony Balls and Stone, and I want you to go over and get that teacher broad, and I want you to cut her heart out and hang her up by her toes. Got me?"

"Yes . . . but—"

"But? But? No buts. The only but you better worry about is your butt, what's going to happen to it if you don't do as you're told. But! Butmyass. Some fucking shithead asshole Superman you turned out to be." The Clyde dummy turned its head with a creak and looked up into the horrible face of the God of the Razor and shook his head, and the God shook his head from side to side and looked very unhappy, frowned so hard his stickpin teeth poked out of his razor-slit mouth, punched his lips until they bled pops of black blood.

The Clyde dummy held up its wooden arm, said, "Wait a minute. Now just wait a minute. Brian's all right, just a bit fucked over right now. He's not fully awake."

The dummy turned back to Clyde, leaned well forward and said, "This is no dream, Brian old boy. This is the real McCoy, and knock on wood," the dummy rapped wooden knuckles against its wooden chest, "I've told old Razor God here that you're a good man." The dummy leaned so far forward now he nearly fell off the God's knee. He whispered, "You wouldn't let me down, now would you?"

"No," Brian said. "Course not."

"Yeah, course not."

"I just thought I was dreaming, that's all. I mean I didn't know it was really you."

"Right." The dummy leaned back on the God's knee, turned to look the God in the face again. "See," he said. "I told you Brian was an okay guy, didn't I?"

The God made no answer, but a few of the stickpin teeth disappeared into the jaw of his mouth. The face seemed to relax; went from real ugly to just ugly.

The dummy turned back to Brian, said, "Get your shit together, man. Get it together quick like. I'm packing my bags tonight, and I'm going to get everything moved in that hollow head of yours . . . Oh, shall we say, 0600 hours?

"Now, I want to make a few things clear. The God here, he's a pretty patient guy, more patient than me in fact, and you know that I'm a regular fucking saint when it comes to patience. I mean, I never did get around to deballing Loony, and I should have. If I'd done that early on, well I wouldn't be here to talk to you tonight. Not that I mind now, I mean I stretched my own goose on account of some promises the old God here made me. Came to me in my cell and said, 'Clyde, old buddy, have I got the plan for you. Only thing is, you're going to have to come on over here on the Dark Side.' So, I say, what the hell? I mean, what am I doing anyway? And here I am." The dummy spread its hands and smiled.

"So it's pretty nice over here. Beer, pussy, lots of blood. Oh, the blood, Brian, so beautiful. And the power I got, man. I mean, I can do all sorts of neat fucking things.

"I'm running my mouth, I guess. Point I'm trying

to make is you can do your duty and come over here on the Dark Side and live like a fucking king, or you can fuck up and come over here on the Dark Side, only you won't be living like no king, buddy. Nasty stuff over here for fuckups. Like riding the edge of a razor blade forever, feeling it slice up through your balls and belly, but never quite doing you in, just slicing and sawing and . . . Well, we don't need to make that any more clear, do we?''

Brian shook his head.

"You're special to me, Brian, really. I want the best for you, but you got to attend to some chores first, before we lay all this fun stuff on you. Now believe me, I know it can be rough. Boy-fuckinghowdy, can it. I mean, I paid my dues and I remember. I'm not one to forget, pal. So, in the final bullshit of all this, what I'm telling you is, you got to waste the teacher cunt and anyone that gets in the way of you wasting her. Then, when you're all finished, you can think about coming on over here for a big beer party.'' The dummy turned to the God. "Right, G.R.?'' The God nodded its fearful head ever so slightly.

"I understand,'' Brian said.

"Hey, that's good,'' the Clyde dummy said. "Real fucking good.''

"No problem.''

"Better yet. Now listen: Going to be with you on this, right inside your head. I'm you. You're me— sort of. Get my drift?''

Brian nodded.

"Good.'' The dummy suddenly turned his head to the God, said, "What's that, G.R.?'' which surprised Brian because he hadn't heard the God say a word. "Right,'' Clyde said to the God.

"He says we're killing time, but not people. He's right, you know."

The God reached down, picked up the Dark Side Clock dangling on its strand of gut, and held it in front of his face, frowned so the stickpin teeth punched out his mouth again. Then he turned the face of the watch toward Brian.

Brian looked at the watch, at two skeletal fingers that served as hands, noted there were no numbers on the watch, only a face—a real face, his face, trapped inside, squirming and pressing its nose in little wet smudge circles against a smoky glass.

And the God pulled the watch back and looked at it, and for the first time he spoke and it was the voice of thunder and lightning on a scary, electric-storm night, "Bless your soul."

The God dropped the watch between his legs. It swung like a pendulum, scraped the floor and threw up sparks.

Brian moaned, thought: Let me out of this nightmare.

"No nightmare," the Clyde dummy said, as if Brian had spoken aloud. "Least not the kind that goes away. We've got work to do. You can have some time on it, but," and Clyde's wooden face cracked around the mouth and eyes and Brian could see real flesh beyond the wood and Clyde finished the rest of his sentence in a loud, edge-of-a-scream voice, *"I want that bitch! I want that bitch! I want her dead, dead, dead, dead!"* Then in a voice as calm as the eye of a hurricane: "And if I don't get her, guess who gets to take her place? You know him. I know him. His first name begins with B. His last name begins with B. B.B. Ring any bells?"

"I'll get her, Clyde."

"Hey, do I look worried? Never doubted it a minute. I know you will." The dummy lifted its hand and pointed a finger (real flesh punched out of the wooden tip). "I'm you. You're me." More cracks appeared around the dummy's mouth and eyes and one crack widened, ran up the cheek, struck the right eye and exploded it in fragments. Behind it was a very real eye—Clyde's eye.

"I'll get her. I tell you, I'll get her."

"You got no choice—unless you consider eternity with a razor blade up your ass a choice. You see, the God of the Razor is our god, Brian. He's the ruler of all sharp things. Knives, razors and the clean paper cut. I mean, he's our main man. He's going to be there with you when you cut the bitch's heart out—there with us! He's going to guide our hand."

The Clyde dummy suddenly went limp. Pieces of wood fell away from its face. The God of the Razor took off his top hat—and perhaps had Brian not been so frightened, he might have found the bald head with a zipper down the middle amusing—and put the dummy into it. He then put the hat on his head, and Brian could hear clearly the sound of a zipper being unzipped and zipped back beneath the hat.

The God took hold of the gut from which the watch dangled, flipped it into one hand and wound the knob briskly with the other. Brian felt a spring tightening in his brain, tightening to the point of explosion.

"*Tempus fugit,*" the God boomed, and then Brian sat upright like a half-closed jackknife in his bed, and outside the window there was another boom, only it was thunder and not the voice of the

God of the Razor, and it was followed by a hiss of lightning that was not too unlike a cosmic sigh.

Brian realized he had wet the bed like a little kid.

TWO

Next morning Brian tore off the sheets and took them down to be washed, told his mother that they were sweaty. She asked no questions, because none ever occurred to her, and then Brian went back upstairs, and a third of the way up he stopped and listened. He had heard a sound, like the scraping of a chair on a floor. Had it come from inside his head?

"Moving in the furniture tonight . . . packing my bags . . . shall we make it 0600 hours . . ."

Brian ran up the stairs, into his room, to the mirror in the bathroom. Behind his eyes, ever so faintly, he could see Clyde's eyes.

"Got you, buddy," Brian said. "Don't sweat, pal. I'll get it done. You keep that Dark Side beer cooled."

THREE

The Witching Hour.

A cool October night with the wind sighing through the trees and house eaves like multitudes of dying men breathing their last.

Down the street a dark car comes, lights bouncing, motor grumbling.

In front of the Blackwood house the lights and motor die. Doors open, close gently.

A minute later Brian's bedroom glass rattles. Rattles again.

Brian rolls over, listens. He thinks: Is that Clyde scratching at my brain?

Trembling, he sits up in bed.

The window rattles again.

He throws back the covers, puts his feet in slippers and slide-walks to the window.

It rattles again, and he realizes that something is being tossed against the glass. He looks out, sees a car crouched by the curb. He recognizes it.

The glass rattles again.

Brian raises the window, looks down, sees two familiar shapes.

They wave. Brian lifts a hand in return.

He closes the window, dresses, goes down.

FOUR

"Clyde came to me," Brian said to Loony and Stone.

Stone and Loony looked at one another.

"I bet he smelled bad," Loony said, thinking Brian was making a joke.

"In a dream. He says we're to kill the teacher bitch that got him caught. We got to do that."

Loony looked at Stone again.

"I know how it sounds, but this is the real thing. Clyde, he's moved into my head, like it's some kind of doll house, you know."

Pausing, Loony said, "Yeah, sure."

"I know you think I'm crazy, but he tells me we got to do this."

"Don't care if you are crazy," Loony said, then added quickly, "Not that I think you are. I mean you say we got to do this thing, then we'll do this thing. I'm for whatever you say. I like being told what to do. Me, I fuck up too much. And Stone, he likes it too. Huh, Stone?"

Stone nodded.

"You see, Clyde's inside me now," Brian said. "Living in my head."

"Sure," Loony said. He'd been sniffing paint thinner, and nothing sounded odd to him.

"I say we get her soon," Brian said.

"Say when. Tonight if you like."

"No. I'm not wanting to go off half-cocked. We've got to wait until the omens are right."

"Omens?"

"Signs."

"Like what?"

"October twenty-eighth."

"What's with the twenty-eighth?"

"Clyde's birthday. We go then."

"Sounds good to me. One night's as good as the next."

"No. That would be the night. The night of Clyde's birthday. He would have been eighteen. He wouldn't want me to wait any later."

"Twenty-eighth it is."

"Okay then . . . Is someone in the car?"

"Yeah."

"What the fuck you doing with someone in the car? Who is it?"

"Jimmy and his old lady."

"Who?"

"Don't get mad, now. He's been helping us out."

"How?"

"He works at the courthouse."

"I don't want the fucker's life history. I want to know what you're doing with him over here. That's what I want to know."

"He's a friend, I tell you."

"You mean he bought you a tube of glue."

"He works at the courthouse—"

"What's that got to do with shit?"

"I'm trying to tell you. Calm down and listen."

"Make it good."

"It's good. I thought maybe he could help us out, on account of he works at the courthouse. Thought maybe he could give us the inside dope on Clyde, but Clyde hung himself, did himself in."

"He's in my head."

"Well, right. Sure. I mean . . . thought Jimmy could maybe tell us how the jail was set up and all, thought we'd get Clyde out of there, but he hung himself . . . and that was all of that. But this Jimmy, he's been letting us stay with him."

"He know about us? What we did?"

"Well . . ."

"Well what?"

"Well . . . kind of."

"Shithead!" Brian slapped Loony across the ear.

"Goddamnit, man," Loony said. "He's been helping us. He wants to be one of us. I mean Clyde used to bring in different people."

"He had the good sense to choose. You don't."

"He's all right, ain't he, Stone?"

Stone nodded.

"Great, Stone says he's an all-right guy. I mean, that's what I was waiting to find out, if Stone thought he was an all-right guy. I let you two assholes out of my sight for a minute—how long you been living there?"

"Since that night we decided not to go back to The House anymore. Listen to me." Loony moved close to Brian. "You'd be proud of me. This guy is a patsy. He's scared of us. He plays like he's our friend, and in a way he is. He wouldn't do nothing to upset us on account of his girlfriend. We've never told him what we'd do, but I've sort of hinted."

"You've sort of hinted."

"I tell you, he's okay. One more man can't hurt."

"A cunt can hurt."

"She's all right for a girl."

"Christ, Loony. Why didn't you just put a fucking ad in the paper?"

"He's all right. If he ain't all right, I'll waste him myself. Right now. You don't like him, I'll cut his balls off right here, suck the girl's eye for a grape. Right here. Right now. Say the word. Don't even look at them if you don't want. Say kill them, I'll go over there and kill them. You tell me what to do. What you want, that's what you get."

"Let me see them."

"Sure. You don't like them, just give me the word. You say it, I'll do it. Stone's the same. You the same, Stone?"

Stone nodded.

Loony pulled up his sweatshirt. A sheathed knife was stuck in the front of his pants. "Just say it."

"All right, let's meet this Jimmy and his cunt."

"Her name's Angela."

"I don't give a fuck what her name is."

"Just saying."

"Don't say dick, Loony. You're smarter when your mouth is closed."

"Yeah, all right. I don't know dick."

They walked over to the car. A back door opened and a lanky boy with a pimpled face got out. A dark, attractive girl followed him.

"Love birds," Brian said.

They didn't say anything. Angela slid her arm around Jimmy's waist.

"You a spick?" Brian asked her.

"Yeah, I guess."

"You are or you aren't. Which is it?"

"Yes."

"You two want in?"

"Yeah," Jimmy said. "Yeah, we want in."

"What about you?" Brian asked Angela.

She looked at Jimmy. "Sure."

"We play hardball here. You know that?"

"Yeah, we know."

"You don't play the game right, may find yourself fertilizing center field. Know what I'm saying here?"

"Yeah, I know," Jimmy said. "We know."

"That's good. You might be asked to play all positions on this team. First base, catcher, short-stop. Anything we want you to play, you play it. Got that?"

"Got it."

"And her."

"Got it," she said. "I do what Jimmy says."

"No, you do what I say."

"She will," Jimmy said.

"That's good, real good. I like to see a girl that knows her place in the scheme of things. One last thing, now that you're in don't think about flaking out. There aren't enough places to hide or enough police to protect you."

"Got you," Jimmy said.

"You're in then. Now, go ahead and get back in the car. I'm going to talk to Loony and Stone here."

They got back in. Brian walked with Loony and Stone to the middle of the yard.

"What do you think?" Loony asked.

"I don't know. You watch them. They go to the police, something like that, and I'll have your balls to stuff with coffee beans so I can have me a rattle. Got me?"

"Got you. They won't go no place. We'll watch them, won't we, Stone?"

Stone nodded.

"All right. I'm holding you to it. I don't want to

see you guys again until the twenty-eighth. And get a shotgun, and some knives. Be sure you bring the knives, sharp knives. I'm going to cut that god-damned teacher's heart out."

"We'll get the knives."

"You do that. Now, so long. I got to get to bed so I can get to school in the morning."

"School?"

"Yeah, unlike you guys, people know I'm alive and I can catch hell about not going to school. I'm going to keep my nose clean."

"I thought you got expelled."

"So they let me back in. My mother begged some."

"That's shitty."

"Twenty-eighth's my last day. After that, we're blowing up-country."

"Suits us."

"Now, so long."

FIVE

It would be over a week before the authorities found Brian's mother cut to pieces in her bed. And they would find her only because the next-door neighbors had complained about the stink. Since she lived on a retirement check and had no friends, just her "loving little boy," no one had missed her. But it would be determined that she was probably murdered early on the night of the twenty-eighth. Written on the wall in her blood was a note. It read:

> Good night, Mommy. Gone to Hell. Won't be back. Your loving baby boy.
> P.S. Clyde sends his love.

SIX

October 28, 11:30 P.M.

They went over to the apartment where Becky and Montgomery Jones lived, climbed out of the car and stood for a moment in the crisp October air.

"Jimmy, you're going with us. Angela, you're going to stay in the car, be ready to honk the horn if anything comes down we should know about. If that happens you crank the motor and drive over to the stairs so we can get in quick like. Got me?"

Heads nodded all around.

"Let's do it," Brian said. The four of them crossed the lot, went upstairs. Brian pressed his ear to the door.

No sound.

He took out his pocket knife and put it between the edge of the door and the lock and rocked the blade from side to side until there was a snicking noise.

"Easy as hell," he whispered.

They went inside, Brian and Stone and Jimmy with knives, Loony with the shotgun.

Less than a minute later they discovered the apartment was empty.

Except for a cat and Loony picked it up and petted it. "She got herself a cat," he said.

Brian cursed. He looked about. Found on the bar a note that read:

Dear Dean and Eva:

Just throw Casey's litter box out once. Fresh litter under the sink, food is there too.

Thanks so much for feeding him. And thanks for the loan of the cabin once again.

                                        Beck

"Shit!" Brian said. "Gone camping or something."

"They'll be back," Loony said, scratching the cat behind the ears.

"We're not waiting. We're going to find them."

"How?" Loony asked.

Brian turned on the light over the bar, flipped open the little phone and address book there. He found a Dean and Eva Beaumont listed. They lived on Heard's Lane.

"Well," Brian said, "here we are, the Beaumonts. We'll pay them a little visit, find out where this cabin is." He tore the page out of the address book.

After Loony killed the cat they drove over there.

The pot of blood on the stove of Hell had just begun to boil.

PART THREE:
The Shark Shows Its Teeth

October 31 (Halloween)

Somewhere in the United States, someone is brutally murdered every twenty-six minutes.
> —Statistical fact

Fierce as the Furies, terrible as Hell.
> —Milton, *Paradise Lost*

By the pricking of my thumbs,
Something wicked this way comes.
> —Shakespeare, *Macbeth*

ONE

October 31, 12:02 A.M.

—clay road winding, '66 Chevy humming, falling forward in time . . .
And so for a few more miles the car rolled on. Brian driving with his pale face looking ghostlike in the night, the others sleeping, storing up . . .

TWO

October 31, 12:27 A.M.

They found another pasture, Brian stopped the car and Loony got out to open the post and barbed-wire gate.

Brian drove the car through. Loony closed the gate and climbed back inside. They drove through the pasture, past sleeping cows, some of which came unstuck from sleep to look up and watch the black shark sail past.

They found a collection of pines next to a metal enclosure that contained water and had salt blocks placed on the outside and all around. The car stopped and the lights went out.

Brian got out, took a leak. "I'll be back," he said. He walked off.

Five minutes later Jimmy and Angela climbed out of the car, walked off in the opposite direction. They looped over a slight rise in the pasture and found a copse of hardwoods that the fall had shook free of leaves, sat down beneath them, backs to an oak.

"I'm scared, Jimmy," Angela said.

"I know. I am too."

"What are we going to do?"

"I don't know." Jimmy didn't want to admit it, but he was even more frightened than Angela thought. The moment she began to get rattled, show obvious fear, he had begun to rip out at the seams. For all his macho bravado, Angela was his anchor, and when her calm and cool began to slip, the final stitch of his own control began to unravel —rapidly.

"He's crazy, Jimmy. They're all crazy."

"I know."

"By the Blessed Virgin, how did we get into this?"

"Me. Me wanting a few friends. Me the tough guy. I'm not so tough, Angela."

"So, who wants tough. I've grown up with tough. I've seen tough. I want to see gentle. I want to get out of this. Those poor people, Jimmy."

"I know . . . while you were being sick in the hall, Brian, he made me cut the woman . . . She was dead, but he made me take a knife and do some things to her breast . . . I didn't want to, but if I hadn't they'd have killed me . . . and you."

"After they got through with me. Do you see how that Loony looks at me?"

"Yes. I want to kill him, but . . . I'm not tough, Angela. I'm just . . . I just am, that's all."

"We've got to split out of this, Jimmy. That Brian, he's going to kill that woman and I don't even know why really."

"Less we know the better."

"God, he's crazy, so crazy, crazier than the rest. Last night, late, after we'd parked in that other pasture, I got out to go to the bathroom and I found me some trees and it was cool, and I got to thinking how it would be to run, to just take off and not come back."

"You should have."

"I couldn't leave you. Never. I'd die first. So I'm going to the bathroom—got to pee all the time now, it seems—and I notice that just a little ways off, out in the moonlight, is Brian. He didn't see me, and I was frightened, you know, not sure I wanted to show myself on account of I don't know how he's going to act, you know. Maybe he'll think I'm spying or something. So I just sat real still, thinking he'd go on, but then he starts talking to himself, but . . . This was really scary, Jimmy. And I heard him answer himself, but not with his own voice. In another voice, and I swear on the Blessed Virgin," she crossed herself, "the voice that answered him back didn't sound anything like his. The voice made the hair on the back of my neck crawl. It was a human voice, but . . . there was something wrong with it, Jimmy. And this voice, he kept calling it Clyde—I guess that's the guy we've heard them talk about, the creep that hung himself.

"Anyway, I didn't move, just watched. I was really frightened then. And I watched Brian and he started walking back and forth, you know, nervous like, and pretty soon there's another voice, and . . .

it wasn't like a human voice, Jimmy, it was deep
and rumbly and sounded like someone trying to
talk and gargle at once, only it was loud. And I
started to just up and run like a deer, but I'm
scared, you know. I think, this guy is absolutely
Flip City. He's talking to himself and answering in
two other voices . . . But I don't know how he
could make a voice like that last one, and neither of
them sounded like Brian . . . And once . . . I'm not
sure about this, Jimmy. I was frightened and maybe I just thought I heard it, but it sounded once
like Brian, and this voice he called Clyde, were
talking at the same time . . . just for a few seconds, you know, and it was like Brian had ac-
cidentally started talking when Clyde started
talking and when he knew he was doing that he
just shut up and the voice he called Clyde went
on.

"I didn't understand what was being said, least
not much, Brian was too far away, but I heard
something about a razor and about tomorrow night,
and then Brian sat down on the ground—I mean
he just sat, like his legs had melted out from under
him, and then Brian said something . . . crazy,
crazier than anything else. He said, 'Clyde, turn off
that goddamned television set.' I could hear that
plainly, every word of it. It was like someone had a
set on and it was turned up too loud for him or
something . . . So he got quiet then, and while he
was sitting with his head hung down, I snuck out of
there. I tell you, Jimmy, it was scary. He's crazy,
completely Flip City."

Jimmy, who was shivering, said, "I know."

"I think that's where he's gone again tonight. To
go out there somewhere to talk to this Clyde, and
maybe this other voice—shit, Jimmy, you should
have heard . . . I don't know how he could have

done that with his voice. It was like one of those
demon voices out of that movie with the green
puke, *The Exorcist*. Jesus, Jimmy, Jesus and the
Blessed Virgin."

THREE

October 31, 5:49 A.M.

He awoke before the alarm was to ring, looked
where his wife should be, and she was not there.
Only her indentation and the sweet woman smell of
her mingling with the crisp morning air.

Ted Olsen cut off the alarm, cried out,
"Roxanne?"

"Making breakfast," she said from the kitchen.
"Come in here, it's warmer."

He scratched his head and scratched his scrotum
through the slit in his boxer shorts, then he went to
the bathroom to wash up and brush his teeth. He
always brushed his teeth first thing in the morning,
even if he were about to eat. Brushing made him
feel human again, nothing like getting the old
green hair off the fangs. After breakfast, he'd brush
again. He even went as far as to carry a toothbrush
and paste with him while he worked, and two or
three times a day, he'd brush. It was almost a
fetish. Probably because his parents had had such
bad teeth.

He finished his toilet and dressed without showering, went out of the cold and into the warmth of the kitchen, the smell of bacon and eggs, the sight of Roxanne.

Roxanne, Roxanne.

She stood at the stove, spatula in hand. She wore her short blue nighties and the cheeks of her ass showed themselves in a half-exposed, tantalizing manner. Olsen felt a movement in his pants that wasn't pocket change. He checked his watch. Well, it might as well be pocket change. If he'd gotten up just thirty minutes earlier there would have been time. That was the story of his life. No time.

When he was ready, there wasn't time. And when there was time, he wasn't ready. He was thirty-five, for Christsake, and he had to make a schedule so he could go to bed with his wife.

He looked at his watch again and thought about a squeeze play.

Nope, just wasn't time. That asshole Larry would be by shortly, and if it was like yesterday, he'd be early. Perhaps now, with the psycho who had killed Patrolman Trawler running loose, it was necessary for them to team up, but he'd be damn glad when things returned to normal and he had a car to himself.

He picked his gun belt (Roxanne brought it in for him every morning when he was working, which was most of the time) off the back of a chair, strapped it on. It was a silly habit. He still had breakfast to eat, but after all these years in the Highway Patrol, it had become as natural a thing to do as zipping up his fly—in fact, more natural.

Men and their guns, he thought.

He sat down at the table and tried not to look at Roxanne's ass, which was difficult, because as she cooked she wiggled all over the place.

He sighed.

She turned, had a plate of eggs and bacon in her hand. She set it down in front of him and they traded smiles. The toast popped up as if on command (her timing was incredible) and she brought it over to him on a fork. Next she brought butter and coffee, sat down next to him. There was no plate in front of her, only coffee. As usual, she'd eat after he left.

Sometimes he felt a bit guilty about Roxanne and her wifey role. The woman was college-educated and here she was slinging hash for him every morning like a waitress in a two-bit cafe. And all he had was a high school education and a shit-ass, no-thank-you job he'd had since he was in his early twenties. If he applied now he couldn't even get in. You had to have college these days—sixty hours at least.

Truth was, he ought to be cooking for her and she ought to be going to work every morning in one of those classy female business suits or one of those dresses she looked so fine in. As it was, she didn't even have the occasion to wear that sort of thing. For any reason.

Living in the country, with him gone most of the time, or home and just too tired to do anything, wasn't much of a life for an attractive woman. Worse, even, was the fact that his job had grown stale and tiresome, unchallenging.

And now he had Larry.

Crazy Larry. The only reason he was still in the Highway Patrol was the grace of God and friends in high authority—Christ! could a guy like that have friends?

Yesterday, the first time they'd actually worked together, they'd nearly come to blows. The guy was worse than he had heard. Larry had asked him right off what his politics were, and then insulted him and called him a communist when he said Democrat.

Next he'd asked how he stood on "niggers," "spicks," "wops" and other foreigners. And when he explained that he found the terms offensive, he had to submit to fifteen minutes of "it's the nigger-loving bastards like yourself that are bringing the country down around our ears."

If he had to put up with that today . . . Well, he just might shoot the sonofabitch, throw him in a ditch beside the road and tell God he'd died.

For heaven's sake, how could a guy like that walk around loose in society? Here they were combing the country for a nut, or nuts, who had killed a fellow officer, and he was riding with one of the biggest nuts in the country.

"Breakfast okay, baby?"

"Ummm, fine," he said. "Was I frowning?"

"A little."

"Not the food, it's Larry."

"Only been with him one day so far and you're letting him give you an ulcer."

"He is an ulcer."

"Sure sounds like it."

"Just be glad to have it to myself again, my own car. I used to think I wanted a partner all the time, but if it's going to be Larry, I'd just as soon not. When I find out who put me with him, I'm going to strangle them—slowly."

"You think they're still out there, Ted? The ones who killed Jim?"

"They haven't caught them yet. I figure they're in Louisiana somewhere. This area has been combed pretty thoroughly."

"Lot of back roads."

"You're right about that. I suppose if they were

smart enough to hide out somewhere and not panic, they could still be around, but I doubt it."

"Just killed him for no reason."

"Could have been a reason in their minds. Wish it had been Larry."

"Ted!"

"Sorry, shouldn't have said that. Besides, *I'm* going to kill Larry."

"They've traced the car by now?"

"That's the dumb part. Jim called in the license number before he was killed, but there's been some kind of computer foul-up and it won't throw out the owner's name. They can't even find it in the files. Nothing like that has ever happened before, far as I know."

"To think Jim was doing a routine thing . . . and someone blew his head off."

He knew she was talking about him, thinking how it could have happened on his patrol.

"Roxanne, no one is going to blow my head off. I'm getting out of the cop business."

She looked up from her coffee.

"I don't know what I'll do yet, but as soon as I can get that figured, I'm quitting."

"But you love it."

"Not anymore."

"You're just saying that."

"No. I don't know why, but one morning I got up and I just didn't feel that knight-goes-forth-in-shining-armor feel."

"It'll pass."

"No, it won't. That's been months ago. It's only gotten worse. Maybe I've just done all I can do with the job. I don't know. But I don't get the thrill I used to, cops and robbers, you know. It's gone. I just don't like the job anymore, simple as that."

"You're really going to quit?"

"Really."

"You're not just saying that because—"

"You're not responsible. I want to quit and have normal hours and live like a normal human being. Have some kids and not have you worry to death about my coming home to them all the time. Just lead a normal life. Soon as I can, I'm hanging it up."

"No idea what you'll do?"

"No."

"I could go back to work for a while, until you decide."

"We'll worry about that later. I've got to do some thinking in that area."

She smiled. "You better eat your breakfast."

He smiled back and ate.

He was brushing his teeth again when he heard Roxanne call from the kitchen, "Larry's here."

Softly, through toothpaste-foamed teeth, he said, "Bastard."

"Okay," he called to Roxanne. He rinsed his mouth, put his spare toothbrush in a very wrinkled paper bag, dropped his toothpaste in with it.

When he came out of the bathroom, Roxanne was holding his hat. He took it from her and put his arms around her, pulled her lips to his.

"That was nice," she said when their lips parted.

"Yes, it was." He pulled her to him again and they had an instant replay.

"My goodness, Teddy," she said when they moved apart. She reached down and pressed her hand to his erection. "I thought your gun had slid around." She began to massage his penis.

"That's one thing I don't need right now."

"Oh?" Her mouth went delightfully pouty.

"Let me rephrase that. I haven't the time."

"Better."

She kissed him again.

Outside a horn honked.

"Asshole," Ted said. "He's early, you know."

"When you get home we'll make up for lost time."

"Not sure when I'll be in."

"I know that. Whenever you're in we'll make it up."

He kissed her again.

The horn honked again.

"Look, it'll just take me a minute to go out there and strangle him, then I'll come back in."

She grinned.

"Gotta go." He reached out and patted her on the ass as he went out of the bedroom. He stopped, turned. "One thing," he said, "when I quit this job, get into something else, I want you to do something with that degree of yours. I never wanted you to be a housewife and nothing else."

"We'll see."

"Bye, baby."

"Love you," she said, and he went out of there. She mouthed the words silently: "Be careful."

FOUR

Ted went outside, putting on his hat. Larry had the car door open and was standing up leaning on it. He yelled, "Move it, Ted. Let's go."

"Just shut the fuck up, Larry."

"Oh, it's going to be like that, huh? Okay, okay."

Larry folded himself inside the car, draped his arms over the steering wheel and looked straight ahead.

Ted walked around front, glanced at Larry through the glass. He looked like a little kid that had been grounded to his room and his toys locked up in the toy chest.

Ted shook his head. What world did this guy come from? It was like he had just dropped in from another planet and hadn't yet learned the social customs.

Ted opened the door, climbed in with a loud sigh. Without looking at him, Larry started the car, began easing out of the drive.

"Damn," Larry finally said, "you drive me crazy. You're the damnedest person I've ever known."

"Me?" Ted said. "Me?" He liked it so much he said it a third time. "Me?"

"Think I'm talking to somebody in the back seat? Yeah, you."

"Christ, Larry, you're a fucking brainwipe, and you're saying I'm weird?"

"You got weird ideas. You act weird. You like niggers and communist—"

"That's about enough, Larry."

"You and the niggers, that's what's wrong with things."

Ted wondered if he should try pinching himself. Hopefully he'd wake up and Larry would be a dream.

"Larry, let me tell this to you one more—last time. That nigger stuff doesn't cut any ice with me. You believe what you want, but give me a break, huh?"

"Are you a fucking Catholic?"

"What?"

"I said are you a Catholic?"

"What's it matter? You trying to find something else to fight about?"

"Then you are a Catholic?"

"I didn't say that."

"But you didn't deny it."

"No, I'm not Catholic. I'm not even a Baptist. I'm not anything."

"A goddamned atheist. I knew it, a goddamned atheist."

"I didn't say that . . . What's it matter, huh?"

"It matters that I want to know if I'm driving around with a goddamned atheist, that's what matters. I mean I'm laying my life on the line out here, and I want to know how my partner stands on things."

"Go to hell, Larry."

"Hey, that's your place, buddy. You're the atheist."

"I'm not an atheist, Larry. I don't have any interest in organized religion, that's all. I don't believe in having to go to church, that sort of thing."

"I thought so."

Ted hated himself, but he couldn't resist. "What's that mean?"

"It means what you said, you're an atheist."

"I didn't say that."

"Hey, someone did."

"I said I didn't go to church—"

"See."

"That's not the same thing. I just don't like organized religion, that's what I said."

"Means the same thing. You don't like or go to church, you're an atheist."

Ted sighed. "Have it your own way, Larry."

"Hey, you ought to think about God and church, buddy. Made a new man out of me. Before that, well, wasn't much about me that was any count."

"Yeah, well, you're priceless now, Larry."

"Was that some kind of crack?"

"How do you do this to me? We did this all day yesterday. I went home with a headache. Do you do this every time you're tied up with a partner?"

"Do what?"

"Drive them crazy."

"I haven't had that many nigger-loving, commie partners, if you must know."

"Pull over."

"What?"

"Pull over."

"What for?"

"Just pull over."

"Tell me what the fuck for."

"I'm fixing to whip your ass up one side of this highway and down the other."

"You and how many of your nigger buddies? That's what I'm trying to ask you."

"Pull the fuck over, you chickenshit bastard."

"All right, goddamnit, all right, you're gonna wish you'd kept your fucking mouth shut, that's what you're gonna wish, that's what I'm trying to tell you."

Brakes slammed. The patrol car rocked.

Larry jerked his door open, started around the front of the car. Ted got out on his side, proceeded to do the same.

"All right, boy," Larry said, "this is it, the big time, your day in the ring."

Ted kicked Larry in the balls and dropped him. Then like one of the Three Stooges, bent down, took hold of Larry's hat and jerked it down over his eyes and ears.

A car with an elderly lady in it drove around them (for they were only partially out of the highway). She stared, slowed, pulled over and stopped, watched through her rearview.

Well, Ted thought, it isn't every day you get to see two highway patrolmen stop in the middle of the highway to go a few rounds.

He waved the woman on. She pulled back onto the highway, drove away. Slowly.

"Are you all right?" Ted asked.

Larry freed one hand from his crotch and pushed his hat up. "You ask me that with me sitting here ruptured, you ask me that?"

"Okay, you want some more?"

"I'm down here on my knees holding what's left of my nuts and you ask me if I want some more?"

"Then shall we get on with the business of being respectable law officers?"

"Why'd you kick me in the balls, man?"

"It seemed like the right thing at the time."

Larry finally let go of himself, wobbled to his feet. "Don't hit me now."

"Larry, I'm not going to hit you."

"You just did. Kicked me. That isn't manly."

"You pushed me too far, Larry. You're fucking crazy and making me that way. Here, let's shake."

"No way. I'm not shaking hands with the man that just kicked me in the nuts."

"Have it your way. You want me to drive so you can hold yourself?"

"You don't let up, do you?"

"Me!"

"Drive, goddamnit, drive."

Ted got in behind the wheel, Larry on the other side; he sat holding his crotch.

Ted glanced at him.

"You didn't have to kick me in the balls, pal. If you hadn't got in the first lucky lick, it would have been rough."

"Yeah, I was lucky."

They drove in silence for a few miles, then Larry said in a surprisingly chipper voice, "Want a Snickers?"

Ted glanced at him. He had gotten a couple of candy bars out of the glove box and was offering him one, smiling. For a fleeting instant Ted wondered if it had a razor blade inside.

"Yeah, I guess," Ted said. "Thanks."

"I love 'em," Larry said.

Ted took the candy. Larry began peeling his.

Ted unwrapped the bar with his teeth and a free hand, took a bite. No razor blades.

He glanced at Larry. Larry was eating as contentedly as a cow chewing cud. It was like the kick in the balls had never happened.

Ted thought: Well, I'll be a sonofabitch.

FIVE

She awoke not long after the dream about the bloody hand. The palm had something bright sticking out of it and there was blood everywhere: the fingers, the wrist.

When she sat up and put her back against the headboard, she realized that Monty was awake, up on one elbow, frowning. "Are you all right?"

She nodded.

"The dreams again?"

"Yes."

He rolled out from beneath the sheets and picked his pants from the floor. She watched him, really seeing his body for the first time in a long time. And for the first time in a long time, she found his maleness stimulating; nothing to scream from the rooftops about, but something.

He pulled on his pants, picked up his shirt and put it on. When he turned, he caught her looking at him.

"Becky, you want to tell me about the dream?"

"It doesn't matter."

"It does matter." He sat down on the edge of the bed.

"It's okay."

"No. It's not okay. Not sure how to say this, but . . . I care. I know you believe that these are more than common dreams, and that I'm . . . Well, I'm not trying hard enough to understand. Believe me, I am trying. But try to look at it from this side of the fence."

"I have tried."

"What I'm trying to say is this: Can we start over?"

"What do you mean?"

"Start over. Obviously this isn't working. Obviously I'm not handling this right."

She was silent for a moment. Need and desire to please radiated off Monty like heat. She thought about a time not so long ago when she asked him to promise nothing would ever come between them, and he had promised. And now, there was this between them, and it was as solid as a metal wall.

"What do you suggest?" she asked.

"I suggest I listen to you, that you tell me about the dreams. I suggest that when you finish telling me about them, I refrain from trying to explain them in my pop psychoanalyst way."

She smiled. "Monty . . . I know it's hard to understand, really. It's just these things are so real . . ." And before she knew it, she was telling him all about the dreams again, explaining that new things had been added to the old visions. The goblins had been in the dreams for some time, but now there were details, surrealistic details. And there was this new dream about the bloody hand.

"I'm not so sure I'm not crazy," she continued. "Not so sure I'm not losing my mind. But these dreams are not like normal dreams, nightmares. They have a quality beyond that . . . sight, sound, smell, even taste, Monty. I can even taste the night air . . . and most of all, there's a feeling, a feeling of terror, like I'm walking blindfolded along a plank over an abyss, and I'm getting closer and closer to falling off."

"Okay," he said softly. "Is there anything we can do about it? I mean, let's look at it like this: the dreams are real. They mean something. They really are . . . visions. What are they visions of? Let's try to identify them, put a label on them, put them here in the real world and see what we've got."

"They look like . . . demons, goblins, devils . . . I don't know. Maybe the dreams are symbolic . . . We've been over this before." She had a sudden feeling that Monty's concern was in fact just another method of leading her down the psychoanalysis path, but she didn't say as much. Benefit of doubt, old girl. Give him benefit of doubt.

Monty shook his head. "I'll be honest with you, I'm stumped. Nothing is even trying to click up there. I mean the bloody hand, the woman you think is you, are obvious. They represent someone being hurt. But why? By whom? It just doesn't click."

"No, and you've given it at least three seconds or four to click."

"Are we back to that?"

"I'm sorry." She wasn't sure she was.

"Tell you what. I won't patronize and you give me the benefit of the doubt, what say?"

"Okay . . . Listen, Monty. Maybe it is all just in my head. I won't lie to you, this talk . . . I mean me just talking it out, telling it to you, and your listening, without pitying, has helped. Things aren't solved in my head, but I feel better . . . a little bit like old times when we used to sit and talk and solve the world's problems."

"Crazy, isn't it? Solving the world's problems when it's hard enough to solve your own."

"Yeah, crazy."

"Want to talk about it some more, try and think it out?"

"No, not just now. We've made a step, but we won't try to make too many too fast." She reached out and took his hand. "What would you say to us fixing some breakfast?"

"Sounds good."

Rolling out of bed, she slipped off her pajamas, picked up her shirt and jeans.

She turned, holding the clothes before her, and saw the hunger on Monty's face. He tried to smile it away. She continued to look at him, and finally let the clothes fall. "Hey, big guy, want to try a roll in the hay?"

My God, thought Monty, she's actually making with the sex play.

"Sure." Play it slow and easy, he told himself. Slow and easy.

He stood up and dropped his clothes. They crawled under the sheets. He touched her hip and their lips slid together, his erection touched her belly, and suddenly she jerked her mouth from his and screamed.

SIX

"You sure you're all right?"

"I'm all right, Monty. Don't ask me again, you're driving me crazy."

"Sorry. Just worried. Here, drink some more water."

She took the glass he offered and drank. "God, I'm sorry, Monty. Of all times—"

"No problem."

"It was fine until I closed my eyes to kiss you . . . Your lips were . . . It was like that kid was on me, Monty. His lips were your lips (*"Scream and I'll cut your heart out"*) and I could smell his sour beer-breath, and the sheet clung to my foot and it was like the other kid's hands, the one whose face is a blank (*"Hold her, hold her"*), and I remembered how my hands were tied, how this kid was on me grunting, how the other was holding my feet, and it was like time travel, Monty, and I was there again (*"Fight, and I'll cut your throat, bitch"*) and you were him and the sheet clutching at my ankles was the other one. I could smell him, hear that Ray Charles album—did I tell you I had to throw that album away?—feel him pressing against me with his . . . dick."

"I know." (God it hurts, God it hurts, another man's dick.)

"I swear, it's not you. I was even ready for sex, wanted it for the first time in months, but the moment I closed my eyes—"

"I know. Don't let that fret you."

"It's been so long since I made love to you, hasn't it? So long."

(Over three months, but who's counting?) "It's not your fault."

"Hold me, Monty?"

"You know it, baby."

SEVEN

12:35 P.M.

Dinner (Becky insisted on calling the noon meal dinner and the evening meal supper) was tuna fish sandwiches and potato chips with instant iced tea. Upset as he was, it didn't do a lot for Monty's stomach. He was glad when Becky insisted that he do some fishing. He had planned to try out some of Dean's equipment, but so far he hadn't so much as seen it. In his youth he had been quite a fisherman, and it just might be the thing to calm him, organize his head.

He put on a light sweater to fight the cool wind, kissed Becky on the forehead and went out to the shed.

He found the key and got some equipment out of

there, decided to use a clown spinner on his setup. Then he went out to the dock and made a few practice casts. He still had the arm. Timing was a bit off, but he still had the arm, and for that he was grateful. Somehow, it seemed very important that something be like—or at least close to—how it used to be.

Becky found beneath the cabinet (looking through the cabin had suddenly become an obsession with her) a small TV with bent-over rabbit ears clothed in aluminum foil.

Christ, this could be the thing. A mind drainer. She got it out and put it on the drainboard, straightened the wounded ears and pinched the foil into place. She plugged it in, picked up a fuzzy station that seemed to be transmitting from the moon.

Oh boy, she thought, my all-time non-favorite, *Hogan's Heroes*.

But what the hell? She pulled up a chair, fixed herself another glass of iced tea (she had tossed off three in the last thirty minutes) and began watching.

Monty cast the clown spinner.

Becky watched TV.

The black '66 sat in the pasture.

And along the highway, up and down blacktops and clay roads, the law ran around like little blind mice and caught no one.

EIGHT

"You're kidding me. You want to stop at every house along here and ask these niggers if they've seen a car fitting Trawler's description? What're you? Nuts?"

"It's a long shot, but what else are we doing?"

"Look, don't you know it's niggers that killed Trawler?"

"No, I didn't know that. Neither do you."

"Dick to a doughnut that it is. When they catch these assholes they'll be niggers. You think these niggers are going to turn in other niggers?"

"Larry, would you like to go another round?"

"Another round of what?"

"Never mind." Ted decided that when he found who had put him with Larry, they were going to die of slow torture. Maybe he'd pull their teeth out one by one with pliers. That would get him warmed up, then he'd use tweezers on their hair, root by root. "Let's just do it. You don't like it, you can stay in the car."

"Okay, have it your way."

The third house they stopped at was owned by Malachi Roberts. Sitting in the drive, Larry said, "What a nigger shack."

"You going to stay in the car?"

"No, tired of staying in the car."

"Let me ask the questions."

"Hey, I only talk to niggers when I have to."

"Fine."

They got out of the car and walked up to the house, knocked. A big black man wearing khaki work clothes answered the door. He was covered in grease.

"Officers," he said cordially.

"Afternoon," Ted said. "I was wondering if I could ask you a few questions?"

"Suppose."

"It won't take but a minute."

"Ask. But make it pretty quick. I got to get back to the shop. Got a car waiting."

"Shop?"

"I'm a mechanic. Got a little shop down the road there, next to the highway."

"Yeah, I've seen it."

Larry went over and sat on the porch, dangled his feet in the empty flower bed. Ted put one foot on the step and leaned an elbow on his knee.

"The twenty-ninth, two days back, a highway patrolman was killed not far from here. Now, I know I'm talking long shot, but he described the car as a '66 black Chevy. Said it had several passengers—"

"I saw it."

Larry, who had been watching the highway, turned to look at Malachi. Ted said, "Sure? I mean it's been a couple days—"

"I saw it." Malachi went over to a big metal rocking chair that had once been green but was now covered with rust, and sat down. "It wasn't two days ago, though, it was one."

"They'd have been long gone by then," Larry said.

"No, I saw them."

"Tell me about it," Ted said.

"It was the night my wife died. Must have seen that old car about one or so in the morning. Couldn't sleep that night, was out here smoking my pipe. I saw the lights, heard . . . hell, felt that car coming, just like it was some kind of black cat carrying bad omens. When the lightning cracked I saw that car clear as if it was daylight, clearer than it is now. I could see people—if they was people —in it."

"If they were people?" Ted asked.

Malachi, who was rocking slightly and staring off into space, stopped abruptly, looked at Ted. "You can go on and think me crazy, if you like, but them wasn't people in that car, they was evils. Some kind of evils. I could feel it as surely as I can feel anything."

"You're absolutely positive when you saw it?"

"Mister, I can't forget. I'm going to a funeral this afternoon, and I'm trying to do some work to get enough money so I can pay for the burying. I'm burying my wife. Night before last—early in the morning, really—I saw that car drive by and my wife died. You don't forget something like that. No. I'm going to have that night in my head for a long time."

"I'm sorry about your wife."

"Not half as sorry as I am."

"Is there anything else you can tell me about it?"

"It turned off toward Minnanette. That's all I know, except it's evil."

"Thanks. And again, I'm sorry about your wife."

"I've got to go to work. I've only got a couple

hours before I got to clean up and go to the church."

"Understand. Thank you."

Ted and Larry went back to the car.

Ted said, "We got something."

"What have we got?"

"We've got an ID on the car. He saw it."

"He says he saw it."

"It's a possibility. I believe him. You don't?"

Larry hesitated. "Not sure. But he's got his days mixed up."

"Maybe not. Probably not. He knows when his wife died and he saw the car that night—that morning. We just like to think that they're so scared of us that they've been driving like hell all the way to Louisiana."

"So they took a back road, could still be going to Louisiana."

"No doubt, but it was the morning of the thirtieth. That means they hid out a day somewhere. And if he spotted them along here, means they didn't get too far on the twenty-ninth after they killed Trawler. They're not idiots. They're playing it casual."

"The evils," Larry said, trying to adopt what he thought was a comic black voice.

"Well, Larry, they may not be demons from hell, but I'd say they're pretty evil. They blew Trawler's brains all over the highway."

"Trawler was a dumb fuck. He'd gotten in the habit of working with a partner. Things were so dull along here they had to team some of them up to keep from wasting so much gas. The partner was out, and he got careless on account of he was used to backup."

"We're teamed, Larry."

"Only because they think they got some bad boys out here. Bet it wasn't nothing but a bunch of drunk niggers."

"Doesn't matter. We're dealing with some cold-blooded killers, and if that old man wants to call them evils, that suits me fine. Christ, imagine, having to go to work the day you're burying your wife, just so you can pay to have her put down."

"If the stupid fuck had burial insurance he wouldn't have that problem."

Ted shook his head, they drove out of there, toward the cutoff for Minnanette.

NINE

5:20 P.M.

Monty's casting was good, but his catching was bad. So far, nothing. Unless floating weeds counted. He'd nabbed enough of those to weave a basket.

He cast once more, but didn't reel it in. He decided to sit down on the dock and reel. He felt certain he was still good enough to make a good cast sitting down.

When he sat, he threw his left hand behind him and pain jumped into it. Jerking it to him, he felt worse pain. He held the hand in front of him. An old hook, half-shiny, half-rusty, had been lodged in the dock, and now it was lodged in his hand. It hurt like hell.

And Becky's dream came to him—the last one. The one with the bloody hand and the bright, sharp object sticking out of it. For the hook, though rusted, had areas of brightness, and as he held the hand before him, it flashed in the sun.

"Now wait a minute here, now wait just a minute here," he said aloud. Then to himself: My God, this isn't an episode of *The Twilight Zone*, for goodness' sake, get a grip. You'll be talking crazy as Becky.

(*"I could see this hand, Monty, and it was bloody, and something bright and sharp was sticking out of it, and the dream hurt me so bad, and it felt so close to home."*)

We're talking coincidence. That's it. That's all.

He looked at his hand, at the bright object, at the blood.

He dropped the rod and reel, didn't notice that it had slipped off into the water. Standing, looking at his hand as though mesmerized, he began to walk back to the cabin.

He went inside, and though he tried to remain calm, his voice squeaked when he called, "Becky?"

No answer. Only the sound of the TV; a car on TV.

"Becky?" He could see her sitting in the kitchen, the top of her head showing just above the bar.

"Becky?"

No answer.

He went over there.

And Becky looked frozen. She sat stiffly in the chair and there were huge plops of sweat on her face and her eyes were wide and there was a moaning noise coming from her throat.

"Becky, Beck, Beck—?" The TV caught his eye. He turned, looked at it. A fuzzy black and white picture was showing, but . . . it didn't look right. The dark car on the tube looked hazy, unreal. Its motor sounded distorted, like an animal growling, and its headlights looked like bright, round eyes.

The damn car gave him the creeps, had the feel of a horror movie. Yes, that was it, they were showing an old black and white horror movie.

He turned away from the tube, said, "Becky?" He reached out and shook her. "Baby?"

Her eyes jerked open.

"Beck . . ." he started, but behind him he heard Lucille Ball yell, "Waaahhh, Ricky."

He jerked to look at the set. The car was gone. It was the old *I Love Lucy* show and it was in midscene, and in better focus . . . But how?

"Monty," Becky said, "your hand!"

TEN

5:49 P.M., and counting . . .

Minnanette was a nice little town; didn't have trouble; didn't know pain. Oh, it had wild kids now and then and maybe they'd get in a fight or drink a little too much beer, but nothing that could really run the rest of the world a good race—far as violence went.

In all its years of existence, the spiciest thing

known to happen was that Hiram Ryan, ten years back, had put a pistol to his head and tried to blow his brains out over his wife who'd run off with Tully Grishom, an insurance salesman from Tulsa, Oklahoma. But Hiram's aim had been a little off and it hadn't killed him. Hadn't helped him, though. Lived in the Rusk State Hospital. Pop used to say, "It's a shame. Old Hiram, he ain't nothing but a turnip green now."

But after this night, Minnanette would have tales to tell. None of them particularly pleasant.

Pop was sitting in Pop's, at the counter, looking out the window at the fast-falling dusk, thinking: Hope the wife brings me something good for supper tonight. That goddamned Mexican TV dinner from last night is still burning my asshole.

He'd been burping and farting around the store all day. And once he'd gotten embarrassed when Mrs. Banks had asked, "Do you smell that, Pop? Smells like something has gone sour somewhere."

Something had, all right. His guts. But he blamed it on the peanut pattie.

He looked at the clock. His dinner should arrive any minute. After that, just a couple hours until closing time.

Five minutes later Pop got his dinner and a kiss from his wife. Then she left and he pulled back the napkin and found a fabulous meal of fried chicken, mashed potatoes, brown gravy, green onions and iced tea. And for dessert, the clincher. Chocolate pudding with whipped cream. Everything a favorite of his, and he enjoyed every mouthful.

Except dessert. He ended up missing that.

* * *

About the time Pop was sitting in Pop's contemplating his dinner, Moses Franklin was busy cussing his dogs and loading them in his pickup. After he loaded them, he tossed his gun, a bologna sandwich and a couple of beers into the cab, then he looked at the sky and saw that the moon was starting to poke out. He thought: Look out, possums, here I come.

And while Pop was contemplating his dinner and Moses was threatening possums, Minnanette's crew of hell-raisers—least that's how they liked to think of themselves—were getting ready for a few Halloween pranks and lots of beer. There were four of them, all fifteen, and all pretty smashed. They'd been over in Old Man Reed's pasture knocking them back, and now they were ready to soap a few windows, shit on a few doorsteps and throw a few eggs, by God.

They tossed off one more beer apiece, in that manful manner they'd been practicing, climbed into the little white Dodge Dart, said a few healthy "Whoopies" and a couple of good "Goddamns," and were off.

Larry and Ted had made three trips to Minnanette already, each time by different backroad routes, and each time they had turned around in Pop's drive, and each time the old man had waved at them, and they had returned the wave. It looked as if all roads led to Pop's.

It was getting to be a pretty unexciting habit.

Finally, they decided to start back to the highway, go on up the road a bit, stop at a truckstop they knew and grab a bite to eat. After that, maybe they'd cruise another back-road route to Minnanette. Maybe. Ted was pretty anxious to just call it a day. He was tired of riding and Larry was starting in on the niggers, the Catholics and the goddamned commies again. Another hour of that and Ted feared he was going to start alongside Larry's head with the barrel of his service revolver.

So, it was with more than a little bit of relief that Ted pulled into the truckstop thinking of chicken fried steak and catsup-covered french fries.

And Brian and his cohorts, at the first hint of dusk, started out of the pasture, down the back roads, flying high and fast, blowing up country toward Minnanette.

Things were about to get ugly.

ELEVEN

The lights at Pop's came on just ahead of their arrival. They cruised into the drive and Brian and Loony got out.

Pop left his dinner, went outside, looked at them, didn't like what he saw, but said, "Help you boys?"

"Boys?" Loony said. "Boys? Hey, old man, you call an alligator a lizard?"

Pop grimaced. "I call a fart a fart, and what I see is a little fart, that's what I see. Now you little farts turn that piece of shit around and get the hell out of my drive. Right now."

With that, Pop started back to the store and his dessert.

Brian stepped quickly to Pop's side. "Say, old man, that isn't polite."

"Get your goddamned hand off me, sonny, unless you want to take to wearing it in a sling."

"You're tough for an old dried-up turd," Brian said.

The old dried-up turd turned and hit him with an uppercut in the gut. Brian went to one knee wheezing.

Loony came out of nowhere, hit Pop in the head with his fist, knocked him down.

Brian stood up, one hand on his stomach. "You're going to wish you hadn't done that, old man."

"Am I?" Pop said, trying to get up.

Loony kicked Pop in the head, made him bleed over the right eye.

"Oh yeah," Brian said, "you're going to regret that."

Pop shook blood out of his eye.

"Pull him to the pumps," Brian said.

Loony grabbed Pop by the collar and began dragging him toward the gas pumps. Pop kicked and wiggled, but couldn't shake free.

Stone, Jimmy and Angela were out of the car now.

Stone went to help Loony, and the two of them slammed the old man's back against one of the pumps. Pop sat there, puffing, dizzy.

"Fill up the car," Brian said to Loony.

Loony unhitched a nozzle, went over to the '66 and started filling up.

Brian walked around to Pop's right side and kicked him. Pop tried to roll over on his hands and knees and get up, but Brian kicked him again, knocking him flat.

Then Brian began walking around him, kicking him from time to time. A couple of kicks made the old man fart.

"How about that?" Brian said. "Kick it and it farts."

Loony put the nozzle back into the pump, said, "Filled up."

"Give me the gas thing," Brian said.

"What?" Loony said.

"The nozzle, shithole."

Loony jerked it free of the pump, handed it to him.

"Stone. Jimmy. Hold him."

Stone went over and grabbed the old man, rolled him on his back. Then, sitting on the ground, he was able to pull Pop's head and shoulders into his lap by applying a full nelson.

"Jimmy?" Brian said. "Don't just stand there."

"No," Jimmy said. And for a moment, he couldn't believe his own voice.

"What?" Brian said.

"You do what you want," Jimmy said. "I'm not going to try and stop you—"

"Course you ain't," Loony said.

"—but you do it. Me . . . Me and Angela, we don't want any part. Just do your thing, but I'm not hurting anyone. Not me."

"Hey, you're fucked," Loony said.

"No," Brian said calmly. "It's all right. I understand."

"We're not going to tell nothing," Jimmy said. "Promise."

"Nothing," Angela said. "We just want out."

"Okay," Brian said.

"Hey," Loony said, "you're fucking me, ain't you? Come on, Brian—"

"Shut up, Loony. I'm still running the show here. They say they won't talk, they won't talk. They promised." He looked at Jimmy and Angela. "Am I right? You promised?"

They both nodded.

"See, Loony. Now, you get over there and help Stone hold the old man."

"You going to let them get away with that?" Loony said. "You said—"

"Loony, do as I say, while you're still able to do anything."

Loony's mouth opened, but the look on Brian's face held him silent. A nervous tic had begun on Brian's lower left cheek and it was rippling wider and wider, beginning to look as if something were moving beneath the flesh.

Loony scuttled over to the old man, and after getting kicked in the shin a couple of times, managed to get hold of Pop's feet. Loony sat down on the ground and held one sticklike leg under each arm.

The tic in Brian's face had ceased. He said to Jimmy and Angela, "No problems."

Brian turned to Pop.

Pop yelled for them to let him go.

Brian walked over and squirted gas from the nozzle, sent it splattering onto Pop's chest. He bent, took hold of Pop's jaws and pinched them. Pop's false teeth came loose, and with a cautious thumb and forefinger, Brian plucked them from his mouth and tossed them.

"Bastard," Pop managed.

Brian jammed the nozzle in Pop's mouth.

"Afraid you're going to have to put this on our bill, old man. Fill her up!" Brian squeezed the nozzle, sent a stream of gas down the old man's throat.

Pop's head jerked from side to side, but he couldn't shake the nozzle free. Brian gave him another squirt. Gas boiled out of the corner's of Pop's mouth and ran down his cheeks, chin and neck.

Brian jerked the nozzle out, splattering gas all over Stone and Pop.

Pop turned his head to the right and began vomiting. Stone released his grip so that the puke wouldn't get on him. Pop rolled on his stomach and continued to throw up and cough.

Brian knelt down by Pop. "Old man, I'm going to ask you a question. I'm looking for this teacher. A real good-looking bitch. Probably has her hubby with her. I had this fellow draw me a map of how to get here, where this place is, and he gave me the area of this cabin I'm looking for, but can you get this: he forgot to pinpoint it for me. I mean, I could be looking through cabin after cabin before I found my teacher, you know. Now this fellow was in a bit of a bind when he was putting this map together for me—Loony, weren't we carving on his wife's tits about then?"

"Ears," Loony said.

"My mistake." Back to Pop. "Anyway, you see our problem here. This couple, they're staying in one of the cabins on Lake Minnanette, and this cabin belongs to the Beaumonts, and I just bet you know them, and know the cabin. Am I right, old man?"

"Fuck you," Pop said.

"Have it your own fucking way."

Brian pushed Pop flat, face-first into the drive.

He stuck the nozzle down the back of Pop's pants, began pumping. In seconds Pop's trousers were sodden.

Standing, Brian tossed the nozzle aside. He reached into his pockets, fumbled around. "Loony, Stone, you got a match?"

Pop tried to push up and run, but Brian skipped to him and kicked him with all his might in the stomach. Pop dropped to the ground and Brian kicked him again. A rib cracked loudly.

"Lie still," Brian said.

Pop groaned, quit trying to rise.

Loony brought a booklet of matches over. Brian took them, said to Pop, "We're going to play a little game, old man. I used to catch armadillos around the house once in a while, and I'd get me some gas out of the lawn mower can and I'd put it on their ass and let them go and I'd chase them tossing matches. Never had one armadillo get away from me. Know what I'm saying?"

Pop had gotten to his hands and knees, the cracked rib felt like a knife blade in his side.

"We're going to play that little game I used to play with the armadillos. You're the armadillo. One for the money—"

Pop got up and ran.

Brian flicked a match at him, yelling, "Cheater."

It hit the old man in the back, bounced down to the seat of his pants and they burst into flames. The fire licked up his body like a torch. His face and head caught on fire from the gasoline that had been spilled there. His shirt leaped into a blaze. He ran zigzag-crazy, screaming. Finally he fell to the ground rolling, tossing along the cement drive like a fish flopping on dry land.

"Cute, ain't he?" Loony said.

"Precious," Brian said. He turned to Jimmy and Angela. "You two, go in there and get something for us to eat and drink. We're moving out."

Jimmy glanced at Pop tossing on the driveway, keening like a rat in a trap. "Sure," he said. He turned to Angela. She was leaning against the Chevy, vomiting.

"You're gettin' it on the goddamned car," Brian yelled. "Get the fuck away from there."

"I'm getting her," Jimmy said. He put his arm around her and eased her gently from the car.

"Get the stuff, like I told you," Brian said.

"We're going," Jimmy said, and he began leading Angela toward the store.

When they had disappeared inside, Loony said, "What about them, you aren't going to just let them go, are you?"

Brian glared at him. The flesh at the corner of his mouth jumped, and then his whole face began to tic, thumping and rippling like a frantic rat trapped in a leather sack.

"What do you think, Loony?"

"They get theirs?"

"Right, they get theirs—when I'm ready. I'm not ready."

They looked at Pop. He was lying still now. Flames were rolling from his back, all the way to his shoes. Smoke was curling up into the store lights, like an escaping soul.

Brian turned to yell at Stone, "You're driving for a while."

Stone nodded.

"Loony, go in there and hurry them up."

Loony trotted for the store. Two minutes later Jimmy and Angela came out, and behind them came Loony. He had his hands full of Halloween masks. "Hey," he said, "look here at these. Ain't tonight the night?"

"Get in the car," Brian said, and the trio ran past him.

Brian ran inside the store. Moments later he came darting out. Behind him, licking from the doorway like forked tongues, were flames.

TWELVE

"Come back here, you sonofabitch," Moses Franklin yelled.

The black and tan hound disappeared into the darkness. Moses could hear him rattling in the bushes, and then he was gone.

"You goddamned sonofabitch," Moses yelled. "I'm gonna blow your ass off when I catch you!"

He was pissed, really pissed. Hundred and fifty bucks he'd paid for that dog at the Canton Trades Day, and the sonofabitch didn't know any more about hunting than he knew about baying at the moon.

The other two hounds came bounding through the bushes, tongues wagging. But not the black and tan knucklehead, he was out running wild.

Moses turned up the beam on his helmet light, and with a sigh, set out in the direction the dog had taken. His hounds trotted alongside.

He looked down at them. They weren't so hot either, far as hunting went, but least they came when you called. If you were going to have a dog, the flea-bitten sonofabitch ought to know its place.

Crashing through the brush, calling for the dog, getting no answer, he resorted to his hunting horn. He was lifting it to his mouth when he saw something out of the corner of his eye.

Redness.

He squinted. What the fuck? That was the direction of the main road and . . . Pop's.

By God, Pop's was on fire!

Swinging the strap on his rifle over his shoulder, putting the hunting horn back in his belt, he began to walk briskly in the direction of the flames, pushing and swatting the undergrowth out of his path.

The dogs bounded along behind him.

From a tall oak, a possum watched in silence as they went.

Down the dark clay road two cars moved. One car was a Dodge Dart. The other a black Chevy. The Dodge was in front of the Chevy by several miles, but it wasn't moving as fast. The kids inside the Dodge were drunk and happy. The kids inside the Chevy were high on fire, blood and hate—except Angela and Jimmy, they were high on fear.

Sam Griffith, the ugliest and the drunkest of the Dodge's occupants, tossed out a beer bottle; tossed it high and backward. The bottle sailed upward, flashed like a quick, silver-toothed smile in the moonlight, fell into the middle of the road, bounced twice, lay still.

The Dodge turned left down a narrow road. Griffith said he knew some good lake cabins they could egg down that way.

The Chevy roared on, hit the bottle Griffith had tossed, whipped it from beneath its rear left tire

and tossed it backward thirty feet. The beer bottle
shattered into three large sharp fragments.

And Ted and Larry, full of chicken fried steak
and too much coffee, were driving toward
Minnanette again, this time by the obvious route.
From Minnanette they were going to make a few
back roads then call the area off, try elsewhere.

"God, God, oh God," Moses screamed.
The store was a writhing monster of red, yellow
and orange flames. It spit black smoke to the sky.
Pop was little more than a charcoal stick in the
driveway.
"God, Jesus, God," Moses kept saying. He went
over to Pop, bent down.
"God, Jesus, Pop?"
One of Pop's hands lifted, slightly, like a dying
butterfly, flopped back on the cement.
"Oh God, Jesus, God."

Ted and Larry saw the flames standing hot and
tall above the pines.
They made a curve. The store—what was left of
it; a charred wood skeleton being devoured by a
fire blob—was visible now. A man crouched over
something in the drive. Ted put it to the floorboard,
screeched into the driveway.

The kids in the black '66 were nearing the cutoff
that led to the cabin where Becky and Montgomery
Jones were, but they didn't know it. Brian was
cursing himself for killing Dean Beaumont too
soon. He thought he would have gotten better
directions if he had waited awhile longer before
starting in on his eyes.
No matter, they'd find them, if they had to turn

down every goddamned road in the country. At least he was certain of one thing: they were close. He'd gotten that much out of Beaumont before he died. The cabin was nearby.

"I didn't do anything," Moses said.

Ted took the rifle from him. "Doubt you did," he said.

"Tell us about it," Larry said.

"I was up there in the woods, hunting, looking for one of my dogs," he waved a hand at the animals who were sniffing about nearby, "and I saw the flames. Came down here and found Pop like this."

"Those pumps might go," Larry said in an offhand way.

"Is he dead?" Ted asked Moses.

"He moved his finger when I said his name."

Larry went over to Pop, squatted down in front of him. "Wheee, burnt to a cracker," he said.

"For heaven's sake," Ted said. "Shut up, will you?"

"Say, just take a look at him."

A dog came over to sniff at Pop. Larry slapped him with the back of his hand. The dog yelped once and slunk off.

Ted knelt down by the man-thing's charred head, asked, "Can you hear me?"

One finger lifted, tapped the drive.

"We're going to move you. Too close to the pumps. Got me?"

The finger lifted again, fell.

"Larry, get his feet." Ted swung Moses' rifle onto his shoulder.

"Move him, he'll come apart," Larry said.

"Don't move him, and he gets blown apart maybe. Us too."

Larry took hold of Pop's feet. He could feel the heat through the charred shoes, socks and flesh. A bit of all three came loose and stuck greasily to his hands.

They carried him off the drive and out into the dirt. They were about a hundred feet from the pumps now. Nothing great, but better.

Moses came over to stand by them, said, "God, Jesus, God."

Ted and Larry picked the fragments of cloth and flesh from their hands.

"Shit stinks," Larry said.

Ted looked at him and shook his head.

Ted knelt at Pop's head. "We're going to pull the car around here and load you in. I wanted you away from the pumps so we could take our time getting you comfortable. I feel a bit safer out here. I think we better haul you to the doctor, on account of . . . Well, you're pretty bad off and an ambulance would have to get here first—"

The old man tried to speak. It was a harsh, painful sound.

"Just take it easy," Ted said.

"Kids," Pop said.

"What's that?"

"Kids," Pop managed again.

"Listen, just take it easy, I'm going to bring the car around."

Ted went to the car. Larry squatted down, bent, looked into the black, ruined face. "Who did it, nigger kids?"

Pop moved his mouth, but nothing came out.

"Try again," Larry said.

"Black Chevy," Pop said quickly, harshly.

"Kids in a black Chevy?"

Pop tapped his finger in the dirt.

"All right, got you."

The finger tapped in the dirt again.

"What is it?"

"Trying to kill . . . couple." The words were coming harder now, were more difficult to understand.

"The kids?"

The finger tapped.

"Got you."

"Beaumont . . . cabin," Pop said, and the words were like rasps on cold steel.

"What's that?"

"The Beaumonts, that's what he means," Moses said. "I've met them a few times."

"How's that?"

"Lake cabin, they've got one. That's what he's talking about."

"You know where this cabin is?"

Moses nodded.

Ted drove the car around, got out.

"Look here," Larry said to Ted, "this guy said some more stuff."

"And?" Ted said.

"About some kids, and a cabin. How they're going to try and kill a couple there, something like that. I couldn't hear him too good."

"Maybe he's delirious."

"I don't think so."

Larry, who had stood while talking to Ted, squatted back down. "Hey," he said to Pop. "Hey, you still with us?"

No movement.

Larry reached over, touched the burned flesh around the neck, felt for a pulse. There was none.

"Cashed in," Larry said, and stood up.

"With those burns, it was probably best," Ted said.

"God, Jesus, God," Moses said.

"This guy," Larry said, "Nimrod the hunter. Says he knows where this Beaumont cabin is."

"Beaumont cabin?" Ted asked.

"That's what the guy said. Something about the Beaumont cabin. He says," he pointed at Moses, "he knows where it is."

"That right?" Ted asked.

Moses nodded.

"Get in the car," Larry said to Moses, "we're going after them."

"We can't do that," Ted said, "he's a citizen."

"I am," Moses said. "Always have been a citizen."

"You want the guys that done this or not?" Larry asked.

"Sure . . . We can just get directions from . . . What's your name again?"

"Moses."

"Uh-uh," Larry said. "I want to be sure I get there. We'll let Moses out before we get there."

"I don't like it," Ted said.

"Me either," Moses said.

"Look at this poor fucker," Larry said, pointing at Pop. "We can't just let kids get away with french frying folks."

"Suddenly you're sentimental, Larry."

"We're the good guys, they're the bad guys. I say we blow their black hats to hell."

Ted looked at the burning building, the flames had licked the wooden flesh from its wooden bones. He looked down at the charcoaled mess that had been a man.

"All right," Ted said to Moses. "Get in the car, and take that stupid light helmet off."

"I don't like this," Moses said. "What about my dogs?"

"To hell with your dogs. Get in the fucking car," Larry said. Then looking at Ted: "Why don't you give him his rifle back, for insurance."

Ted nodded wearily, handed it to Moses.

Ted opened the back door. Moses climbed in, tossed the light helmet in the seat and put the rifle across his knees. Ted closed the door.

"You get to take credit for this, anything happens," Ted said.

"Gladly. Come on, I'm driving. You call in the fire department and a meat wagon . . . There's still the pumps that might go."

They got in the car, Larry behind the wheel. He cranked the engine, looked out the window at Pop's body. "We'll get 'em for you, fella."

Moses said, "You got to take this road a bit, then we'll do some turning later."

They pulled away from the flames and onto the road. Ted picked up the radio mike, called in the location of the fire and the body.

"Sound the trumpets," Larry said. "Here comes the goddamn cavalry. Look to your asses, black hats."

THIRTEEN

"Oh, Monty, don't move. I've just about got it."

Becky had used wire cutters from the shed to cut the tip off the hook, and she was working the rusted thing out now. She tossed the hook fragment into the bar ashtray, poured alcohol on the wound.

"Just like the dream," Monty said. "And the TV . . . what I saw was part of the dream you told me."

"Couldn't be. On the TV?"

"I'm the one talking the loony talk now and you're telling me I'm crazy. We've got our roles changed around. I tell you though, I saw this car you told me about on TV. Did you see it or not?"

"I was just sitting here, watching *Lucy*, and suddenly I felt this thing in my head, like something wiggling, and then the next thing I know I'm looking at your bloody hand—"

"There's some sense to it," Monty said, interrupting. "If you're some kind of receiver . . . and there's something sending out there, whatever sends these messages to you . . . Maybe the TV picked them up, just like you picked them up—"

"Bounced through my head and into the TV?" Becky said without humor. "Old Beck, the satellite receiver."

"And maybe I was imagining it. The hand part had come true, so vivid, like the way you told me in your dream . . . You were in a trance when I came in, I glanced at the TV . . . maybe the channel had some kind of difficulty and another show was sticking in, that's why it was so fuzzy."

"Makes sense," Becky said. Then she laughed. "This is nuts. Now I'm the straight man, trying to make you realize you're hallucinating. I said if I were in your shoes I wouldn't do that." She paused for a long moment. "Monty, the dreams are real. Maybe you did see something on the set. Whatever, you did hurt your hand, like I said. Clyde hanged himself just as I dreamed. If those things came true, then the others will come true. The woman I saw—"

"Now hold on—"

"—was me, Monty. She was dead and hung up by her feet and it was me, I know it for sure."

"You don't know that."

"Yes, I do. The goblins—"

"There are no such things as goblins."

Becky smiled. "Back and forth," she said, "we change roles back and forth. There was no such thing as a person who could dream the future either, remember?"

Monty was silent for a moment, then: "Maybe these are warnings. If I had understood your dream was about a hook in the hand, and if I had believed your dream, I probably could have avoided the hook by not going fishing."

"And maybe you can't change the future. Maybe you wouldn't have known it was a hook even if you had believed. I couldn't tell it was. All I saw was the hand, the blood."

"Listen here. We're not going to submit to this, whatever it is."

"I'm going to die," she said softly. Her eyes seemed to glaze over.

He could see that she was on the edge of hysteria. In fact, he was on the edge of hysteria. Calmly, he said: "If you lose your head, you just might. But if we keep calm, we can whip this. It may be nothing more than our imagination and we can laugh about it later."

"The dreams are not my imagination."

Pushed the wrong button, he thought. "We're going to keep calm. Now, from the way you described the dream to me, there was the car, and

there were trees and a lake. Whatever is supposed
to happen will happen here—if there's anything to
this. So, simple. We leave. Right now. Don't get
anything, just come on and let's go."

"Monty . . ."

"Now. Let's go, come on. Try to recall everything
you can about the dreams, as vividly as you can.
Tell me as we drive. The more you can warn us
against, the better chance we have avoiding it."

He took her arm, and as he led her out, he began
to feel silly. It had crept up on him suddenly. The
stuff he'd been rattling was crazy. Christ! He was
going off his bean, going the way of Becky.

For a moment he thought of changing his mind,
but he remembered the TV, the car.

Silly, goddamned silly. How could it be on TV?
That's the dumbest idea ever.

But the more he thought about that car, Becky's
other dreams, the less he thought of going back
to the cabin. In fact, they left so hurriedly they
forgot to lock the door and they left the lights
on.

FOURTEEN

Dark now. The moon riding high in a cold, clear
sky. The wind playing music in the tops of the
pines. The '66 Chevy pushing shadows to flight
with its bright headlights.

* * *

Monty cranked the Rabbit, backed it around, drove out to the road, headed for Minnanette.

The Highway Patrol car was blowing fast. Larry was grinning. Ted was gripping the seat. Moses had his head down between his knees, saying, "God, Jesus, God."

Monty drove fast while Becky detailed the dream to him again. And then she stopped in midsentence, said: "That's it. That's it, Monty."

"What?" He glanced at her. She was pointing at the headlights coming toward them.

And suddenly Monty knew what she meant. In fact, it was the TV image: a dark car with lights zooming toward them.

"Hey!" Brian said as the Rabbit passed them. "That's the cunt's car." He yanked the wheel. Clay became dust and puffed up in a dark cloud, and the Chevy rolled out of the cloud and was in pursuit of the Rabbit before the dust began to settle.

Monty could see the lights in the rearview mirror, closing fast. He pushed so hard on the accelerator that needles of pain traveled up his leg. The Rabbit was rocking, knocking.

The Chevy was closing.

"I'm the one that cuts her heart out," Brian said.

The Highway Patrol car was closing, and soon they would be near the Rabbit.

Or would have.

But Larry didn't see the broken beer bottle fragments in the road. The car rolled over the glass and a tire blew. The car was doing seventy. It fishtailed and spun and the clay dust flew and the car made a complete circle, fishtailed again and went halfway off in a bar ditch.

Larry opened the door, stepped out into the dust, said, "Damn."

The Chevy was alongside the Rabbit, seeming to coast. Monty glanced to his left, saw the wild, moon-eyed Loony Tunes looking at him.

"Why?" Monty said aloud. "Why us?"

The Chevy eased over to them, bumped the Rabbit ever so lightly. Monty could hear Loony laughing; the chuckles bounced along in the wind like living things.

Monty glanced at his dash lights. Something was going wild—the heat light was blinking like an airstrip landing lamp.

He glanced at the Chevy again. The guy on the passenger side had a gun—a shotgun, he was leveling it.

Monty slammed on the brakes, the car skidded. The Chevy shot past them like a bullet. Becky went forward, hit the windshield. When she tumbled back from the blow there was blood on the glass. Monty glanced at her face. Her nose and lip were bleeding.

No time to worry now.

He jerked the Rabbit into reverse, backed in a short, sharp circle, floorboarded it back the way they had come.

Already the Chevy had turned around and its lights were filling the rearview mirror.

The patrol car had blown the left front tire. It was off in the ditch in such a way that the front tires were dangling, not quite touching ground.

Moses, who was bleeding from the nose and holding a handkerchief to the wound, said, "Now what?"

Ted stood with his hands on his hips, thinking.

"Jack it out?" Larry said.

"I don't think so . . . What might work is to go ahead and change the tire, then push it off in the ditch."

"In the ditch?"

"Push it off until the wheels touch, then try driving it forward—"

"Into the ditch?"

"Sure as hell aren't going to drive it backward, no traction. Might pull into the ditch and hard right along the edge. It gets narrow down there, could possibly pull back on the road."

"Going to have to make an awful sharp turn before the trees . . . if it comes out of the ditch."

"Got any better ideas? If so, I'm ready to listen."

"Nope."

"Then?"

"Let's change the tire and give it a try."

The Chevy was closing again, whipping around to the side of the Rabbit. Monty doubted the same trick would work twice, but perhaps another trick.

He whipped to the left, using the advantage of the small, maneuverable car to point the nose at the Chevy. The Rabbit hit the Chevy just behind the right fender and the momentum of Monty's whipping action carried the '66 to the left, toward the bar ditch.

Monty knew that if the driver reacted in time, could whip to the right soon enough, the weight of the car would be more than a match for the Rabbit.

But the Chevy's driver did not respond soon enough. The black car was at an angle, the rear end whirling around, and Monty was driving it straight for the ditch on the left-hand side.

Nearly there.

Come on, baby. Nearly there.

Just a bit more, Volkswagen, honey.

There!

The Chevy's left tire went off in the ditch, and Monty jerked the Rabbit back on the road. But the car was not without damage. The manuever had smashed the front of the Rabbit good, and the tail end, which had swirled around and smacked the Chevy, was also dented badly. But it was a small price to pay for freedom.

"By God, I beat them," Monty screamed. "I beat 'em!"

Monty made a curve, but not before a glance in the rearview mirror told him the trick had not been entirely successful. He had not pushed the Chevy far enough. It had gained enough traction to reverse out of the ditch.

And they were coming again. Fast.

Larry and Ted had the tire changed now, and with Larry at the wheel and Ted and Moses pushing at the back, they were ready to rock it off in the ditch, hoping the front tires wouldn't bog and that they'd be able to pull out, around, and back onto the road.

Larry cranked the engine to life, yelled out the window. "Hit it!"

Moses and Ted put their backs into it, pushing.

Monty made the curve. The Chevy's lights went out of view.

God, he thought, we're almost back at the cabin. He jerked a look at Becky. She was white as a sheet and the moonlight made her look worse. She had wiped the blood from her face with her sleeve, but it was beading up again on her forehead and under her nose.

"Okay?" he asked.

She didn't answer.

There was a cutoff coming up. It was the one just before the Beaumont cabin. He decided to take it. Maybe it led to some house. Some kind of help.

He took the turn.

But not before he saw a wavy fragment of the Chevy's head beams making the curve. And if he had seen them, chances were they had glimpsed his taillights just before he made the turn.

Pine tree shadows clustered on the road like great, black spiders that seemed reluctant to flee before his headlights.

A shiver ran up his back. He thought: Pines. The lake. He glanced at Becky's face. Her nose and lip were covered with blood again, her forehead wore a band of it. He remembered what she had said about a woman hanging upside down, bleeding.

"Becky," he said sharply.

She didn't answer, just looked straight ahead, her face a growing mask of blood.

The patrol car's front tires hit the ditch, spun, mud flew, and the machine's rear end swiveled to the left, then back.

Traction was finally gained, and the front tires, acting like the front toes of a scrambling sloth, pulled the car forward.

The front end came out of the ditch, and the rear end, clearing the rise, plunged down to take its place. The back wheels hit the mud with a plop, buried halfway to the hubcaps.

Larry kept gunning it.

The tires dug in deeper.

"Hold it!" Ted yelled. "Hold it, goddamnit!"

* * *

The road narrowed, and suddenly Monty felt he knew what was around the curb. A dead end.

He was right.

There was a sudden end to the road. Pine needles took the clay's place. There was a picnic table, trees, and beyond that the lake.

He had trapped them.

"Get out of the car!" he yelled at Becky.

"It's no use. We're dead . . . I'm dead."

He reached over and back-handed her. "Get out of the car. Do you hear me, bitch? I'm scared to fucking death, I don't need you to drop the liberated role now. Get the fuck out of the goddamned car or they won't get to kill you. I'll do it!"

Becky opened the car door, dream-stepped out.

Monty jumped out, ran around, grabbed her arm and began dragging her to the left, toward a dark swath of trees.

"Run, goddamnit, run," he yelled.

She did. Her arm came free of Monty's and she was moving ahead of him, and it was all he could do to stay within three feet of her. He remembered what she had once said about the track team.

Lights pounced on them—the Chevy's lights.

And then they were clawing, stumbling, running their way into the stand of trees, the brush, the ruthless vines.

They could no longer see the lights, but Monty could hear the car doors slamming, and could imagine that the kids were running after them— and at least one of them had a gun, a shotgun.

Monty saw lights through the trees. A house.

"Run, goddamnit," he said, even though Becky was pushing well ahead of him, slapping vines and small limbs out of her path. More than once a limb she had bent aside came back to whip him. He began to run with his arms up, looking between them.

Suddenly they were out of the trees and the lights were bright and the house was there in the moonlight. And Monty might have laughed had it not been so goddamned crazy.

It was the cabin, of course. They were right back where they had started from, ready to shake bloody hands with Becky's dreams.

Monty jerked a look over his shoulder.

Nothing. They weren't pursuing.

That fact failed to be encouraging.

"Get in the cabin," Monty panted. "I'm . . . going to grab something out of the toolshed, something to fight with."

Becky kept going, but when she reached the cabin door, she stopped, turned to look at Monty. He was going into the shed. It was unlocked, the way he had left it after getting out the fishing gear. "Hurry, baby," she said. "Hurry."

He came running out of the shed with a poleaxe and a frog gig.

"It's stuck good," Moses said.

Ted sighed. "Start gathering sticks, rocks, anything you can find to slip under the tires. We've got to build them out of that."

"Any more bright ideas, Ted?" Larry said.

Ted turned, leveled his finger at Larry. "Don't start in on me, asshole, not unless you want to wear the seat of your pants for a hat."

They began to gather debris to place behind the tires.

FIFTEEN

The kids had not pursued Monty and Becky because:

When the five of them got out of the Chevy, Brian had turned to Loony and said, "Grab those two," and he'd pointed at Jimmy and Angela.

Loony waved the shotgun at them and smiled.

Jimmy said, "You promised."

"But *I* didn't," Brian said, and it was Clyde's voice.

"Man," Loony said, looking at Brian, "that's creepy. You sound just like Clyde."

Brian looked at Loony sternly. "I am Clyde, you frigging asshole." The voice switched back to Brian: "And I'm Brian too." Back to Clyde: "See, you fuckheaded dingledick!"

"Yeah, yeah, Clyde . . . Brian . . . You guys."

Stone, his teeth nearly hanging out, was staring at Brian.

"What're you staring at?" Clyde's voice asked.

Stone shook his head.

"Then get these two over to that table."

"Don't hurt us," Jimmy said. "Let us go. We'll just go away, won't say a word."

"Sure you won't. Move it. Over to the table."

"Run," Jimmy said, and he pushed Angela hard to his right, and he bolted to the left.

Stone stuck a leg out, tripped him. Jimmy went

down and Loony stepped over and cracked him behind the head with the butt of the shotgun, knocked him cold.

Stone went running after Angela; caught her before she reached the trees on that side, grabbed her by the hair, and like a caveman with his mate, began dragging her back to the others.

He threw her down in front of Brian.

Brian bent forward, pulled a knife from his belt. "First," he said in Clyde's voice, "we have a little fun."

"Man," Loony said, "that voice is some creepy shit."

Brian whipped around to Loony. "You think this is some kind of fucking game?" The voice was Clyde's. "Huh?"

"No, I just don't see how you do that . . . You do it good."

"You ignorant motherfucker," still Clyde's voice, "we're sharing a head." He tapped the blade against his skull. "See."

"Yeah,"

Clyde's voice: "There's me."

Brian's voice: "And there's me."

Clyde's voice: "But I am the king of this palace. Now, so you stupid fucks won't have to think this over too hard and cause your brains to overload, take the cunt over to the table."

"Please," Angela begged. "Leave me alone."

Stone grabbed her by the hair, tugged her toward the table. She kicked and screamed, but he got her there. Loony took Jimmy by the collar and dragged him over.

Stone still held Angela by the hair.

Clyde's voice: "Do you love this milquetoast?" He waved the blade at Jimmy.

"Don't hurt us," she said.

"Are you deaf?" Clyde's voice asked.

"Do you love this asshole? This is important. There'll be a pop quiz later, so you remember your answers."

"Who are you?"

"I'm asking the questions here," Clyde's voice said.

"Please . . ." she said.

"Last time, for all the apples, do you love this shit?"

"Yes, yes."

"Got a proposition," the Clyde voice said. "I'll let you go if you'll tell me to cut him instead of you."

She looked up at him.

"That's right," the Clyde voice continued. "You say: Cut him, Clyde, cut him up, cut him to pieces, and I'll let you go. Just like Brian made the Beaumont cunt do."

"No . . . No," Angela said.

"Get her up."

Stone just looked at Brian for a moment; the Clyde voice, the way Brian was posturing . . . it was almost too much.

"Has everyone gone fucking deaf around here, get her up."

Stone pulled her by the hair.

"Put her hand on the table, please." The voice was still Clyde's, but oddly gentle, almost kind. Stone recognized that tone; meant something nasty was going to happen, Clyde always did that when he was about to get nasty.

"No, let go," Angela begged.

Stone grabbed her wrist, jerked her hand on the table.

Brian went to the table, moved behind Angela,

ran his hand down the length of her long black hair. Angela trembled.

He leaned over and whispered in her ear: "I've got something for you. Something long and hard and pretty."

There was a long pause, then he said sharply: "This!"

He jerked a fist in front of her face; a knife was clutched in that fist.

"Not what you wanted, huh?" Brian said.

Then the knife was gone, and Brian came around and grabbed her, pushed her face down across the table. He pulled her arm out beside her, and she heard a thunking sound. This was followed by pain.

She twisted her face to see. He had cut off her index finger at the knuckle with one swift chop. He leaned down to look at her face. He had her finger in his hand, pretending to pick his teeth with her fingernail.

She screamed and the scream tapered off to a sob. She passed out. Unfortunately, only for a moment.

When she hazed into awareness, Brian had her middle finger positioned on the table. Stone was helping him by holding her wrist.

Brian leaned his face down to hers again. Her finger was between his teeth, being rolled about in his mouth like a tycoon with a cigar.

"Quick now," Clyde's voice said, "let's hear what you have to say about your sweetheart."

The moon hit Brian/Clyde's eyes and they were as bright and sharp as the knife he held, and behind those metal-bright eyes something bad moved.

"Cut him," she said. "Don't hurt me anymore. Cut him!"

Brian smiled. "Take his pants down," he said to Loony. "Wake him up."

"Yeah, Clyde . . . Brian, whatever the hell," Loony said.

Stone and Loony rolled Jimmy over and unfastened his pants, pulled them down to his knees. Loony took hold of Jimmy's feet and Stone settled at his head, used the palm of his hand to slap him awake, slow and easy, building rhythm.

"Get his underwear down," Brian said, but it was still Clyde's voice.

"By the Blessed Virgin," Angela said, and she began to sob.

Brian stared at her. He hardly looked like himself. His face appeared harder, thicker, darker, the brows looked lower. "There's still time, spick." He showed her the knife. Her blood still dripped from it. "You or him, baby?"

"Him," she said softly, and put her face against the table.

Jimmy was awake now, and aware of what was about to happen. "For God's sake, no. Don't do this, Brian. Please, I'm begging you."

Brian, who looked and walked even more like Clyde now, moved around Loony and stepped between Jimmy's legs.

"God, don't. God, please don't." Then he abruptly began praying. "Our Father, who art in heaven . . . ?"

Brian reached down, clutched with his left hand, and the knife in his right flashed briefly in the moonlight.

SIXTEEN

They heard Jimmy's screams, followed by those of a girl, and though they did not understand them, they felt them to be an echo of their future.

"Monty . . ." Becky began, but if there had been a thought behind the opening, it had died at birth.

"Heat some water," Monty said.

Becky looked up from the chair where she was sitting; she was clutching the axe and there was a sunburst of blood on her forehead, a few rubies of it beneath her nose.

"Heat some water," Monty repeated.

"A little coffee, I suppose?" Her voice rode the line between hysteria and sarcasm.

"Just boil the goddamn water. Get the biggest pots you can find. Fill them, get them boiling. I saw this done in a movie once. They threw water on these guys that were breaking in. Now get with it. I've got to barricade the place."

Becky stumbled into the kitchen area, set to work.

Monty checked the cabin out, made sure all the outside doors were locked. He blocked off the bedroom door with the couch in case they came through the window in there. They'd have a hell of a time pushing the door open with the couch against it. Certainly it would take them long enough that he could defend the area.

He was trying to figure how to blockade the doors that led into the bedrooms when he remembered that one of them contained paneling and carpentry tools.

He went in there and came out with a mouthful of nails, a hammer in one hand and some narrow strips of paneling in the other hand. He stacked it, went back for the rest. It took several trips. He nailed the bedroom doors shut, cutting them off from the rest of the house. He used the rest of the paneling to nail over the windows facing the drive. Only the two large side-by-side windows facing the lake and the one in the kitchen were unboarded now. But at least he would have less to defend, and the kitchen window, being high up and narrow, would be relatively easy to protect.

He retrieved the frog gig, and for a moment felt quite pleased with himself, but the pleasure dissolved when the unprotected lake window exploded and a leathery object came hurtling along with glass shards to land on the living room floor. A voice followed it, yelling, "Trick or treat, assholes."

Becky came out of the kitchen, a hand to her mouth (thinking to herself even as she did it: What a girly mannerism), and saw the glass fragments on the floor and what lay among them.

Even as Monty kicked the object across the room in disgust, she recognized what it was.

Bloody testicles.

SEVENTEEN

"The lights," Monty said. "Cut the lights."

He ducked, moved close to the window, peeped out. He felt for all the world like one of those second-string movie stars in a Western B movie. Next he'd need to finish breaking out the rest of the window with his gun barrel so he could get a good clear shot at the Indians. Only he had no gun barrel—the guns were out there.

A crazy thing was happening out back, between the shed and the cabin. There was this kid and he was capering. He was a strange-looking kid and his body was doing things that were somehow graceful, yet somehow foreign. He had a knife in his hand (flashing from time to time in the moonlight just like his smile) and he was spreading his arms like a heron spreading its wings for flight, closing them, spreading them, and then he would stand on one leg, then two, then switch and stand on the other leg, then two again, and he was laughing.

The kid began to dance toward the cabin, moving at first from side to side, but gaining a bit of ground forward every now and then.

Monty clutched the gig until his knuckles were white.

He looked at Becky. She had picked up the axe and was standing near the front door.

The kid capered closer, stopped:

"Teacher," he yelled, "remember me?"

Monty heard a thud. He looked at Becky. She had dropped the axe, she was shaking her head.

"It's him," she said.

"Him? Who's him?"

"Clyde . . . the one who raped me."

"Get your shit together, Becky."

"It's him, I know that voice. It's—"

"Pick up the axe," Monty said calmly.

"Teacher," came Clyde's voice again. "Want to go another round? It sure did feel good inside you. You got a hot box, baby. I can tell your old man that—"

"Shut up! *Shut the fuck up!*" It had jumped out of Monty's mouth so fast he could not believe that he had said it.

The kid capered some more, spun around on his heel and stretched the hand with the knife and let the light of the moon dance on its tip.

Then he stopped, looked at the cabin, pointed with the knife. "We're waiting, teacher," Clyde's voice said, and Brian's voice continued with: "Hey, buddy, we're going to cut the pretty teacher's heart out."

Monty saw the kid's posture change with sudden drama, and even from a distance, he could see that the expression on his face had altered considerably. Clyde spoke now: "We're gonna cut her cunt out too, asshole. Hear me! Hear me! But not before we fuck her goddamned brains out, and I wanta be first!"

Brian laughing, his voice saying: "We'll be first."

More laughter. (Had it been the stereo sound of dual chuckles?)

Monty blinked. He was losing his grip. What was the point of all this—

A sudden pounding from the front of the cabin explained it. He had been duped by the oldest trick in the book. The others had come up from the other side.

He glanced angrily back at the kid.

He was gone.

Grabbing the frog gig, he advanced toward the hammering, the front door.

Becky, trembling with remembrance of the voice from beyond the grave, picked up the axe.

Monty crept to the door, put his ear to it. He heard a dripping sound, as if great globs of water were falling off the eave of the roof and splattering on the front steps.

Easing over to the window, he bent and found a narrow place the paneling hadn't quite covered. He put his eye to it and peeked out.

He swallowed heavily. There was something hanging from the small front porch roof—a girl. The wind moved her and her head flopped around to look at him. The eyes were wide open and the face was covered in blood. The crotch of her jeans was cut away and her pubic hair was matted with gore.

"What . . . what is it?" Becky asked.

"The girl of your dreams," Monty said.

EIGHTEEN

With wood, rocks and flattened beer cans behind the back tires, Larry was able to free the car, pull it up alongside a barbed-wire fence. Tree limbs scraped at the side of the car as he went, and when the ditch became narrow, almost flat, he crossed onto the road.

Ted and Moses ran to get in.

"As I remember," Moses said, "you hit a stretch of blacktop just before the Beaumont driveway, and it's a long thing. More a short road than a drive."

"Just say when we get there," Larry said, and he stomped down on the gas.

NINETEEN

They put on the Halloween masks Loony had stolen from Pop's store. Brian wore the one with the knife in the skull, the one Monty had thought the most hideous.

Loony, who was embracing the shotgun, said, "Let's splatter them."

"We will. But we're going to do this right," Brian said in Clyde's voice. "Stone, you go up the drive there and find you a place to hang out, just in case we should get visitors. What I want to do to them might take awhile and I don't want to be interrupted. I want this bitch to suffer, like I suffered in that jail cell."

Behind Brian's back Loony looked at Stone and shrugged, put a hand to his head and rotated his finger.

He ceased the action before Brian turned. In Clyde's voice, Brian said, "I've got other plans for us, Loony."

Stone stamped his foot angrily.

Brian turned back to him, and still using Clyde's voice, said, "Don't worry. We'll save something for you. You'll get your fun. Loony, give him the shotgun."

Loony did as directed and Stone took it, began jogging up the driveway, the Halloween mask bobbing loosely on his head.

Near the front of the long drive that led to the cabin, he found a small tree with a wide fork. He climbed into the fork, put the slug-loaded shotgun across his knee and waited.

Five minutes after Stone was positioned, the Highway Patrol car, driven by Larry, made a wrong turn and went down the road where the '66 Chevy and the Rabbit were parked.

Larry cursed Moses for the mistake, and they turned around. But not before Ted got out and used his pocket knife to slash the tires on both cars. That way, the only car leaving this area would be their patrol car.

They backed around and went back up the road,

and made the correct turn into the Beaumont
drive.

Monty and Becky began a system of rotational
checks; moving around the house to each panel-
boarded window, crouching as low as they could
when passing the unprotected lake window.

So far, there were no signs of anyone trying to
break in.

From where they leaned against the cabin, Brian
and Loony had seen the patrol car's lights through
the trees.

They watched in silence until Loony said,
"Who's that?"

"What the fuck am I?" Clyde's voice said. "A
goddamned crystal ball?"

"What do we do?"

"Not a goddamned thing. Not yet, anyway. They
turn down this road Stone will blast them."

They watched the car turn around, watched the
lights go away. And soon after, they saw the car
come into view as it made the Beaumont driveway.

What happened then was:

Moses said he wanted out, but Larry ignored
him. He turned the car down the drive, and Stone,
nestled in his sniper position, raised the shotgun
and fired. The slug hit the right front tire. The car,
which was not moving fast, skidded slightly,
stopped.

Stone fired again. This shot cut through the right
passenger window, hit Ted just in front of the right
ear.

Fragments of glass, brains, blood and skull flew
like a meteorite shower. The slug passed out

through Ted's forehead, tumbled over the steering wheel (passing Larry's face by inches) and exited with a spray of glass out the left vent window, but not before glancing along the metal framing and ricocheting with a clatter onto the hood.

Larry swung the door open, grabbed the riot gun from the back-seat prop, rolled out of the car and onto the ground. Another shot took out the back glass, and Larry duckwalked to the back door (which had no inside levers) and opened it for Moses, who tumbled out uninjured, but dribbling glass from his clothes. He dragged the rifle out behind him by the strap. He was shaking and moaning.

"Is . . . is he dead?" Moses said.

"What do you think?" Larry reached up with one hand to touch something that lay on his shoulder like a grisy epaulet—a wormy grey and red mass of brain tissue. "To live, buddy," he said, thumping it off himself, and almost on Moses, "you got to keep this stuff inside your head."

"Oh shit, Jesus, God," Moses said. "He's going to kill us."

"No, he isn't. I'm going to blow his ass away."

Another slug struck the car. More glass flew, rained down on them where they crouched.

"He's just shooting at the glass because he hasn't any better sense. We take it easy, and he's dead. Now listen here, I'm going to get him. Going to slip off in these woods behind me, cross the road a little farther down, see if I can sneak up on him."

"You're going to leave me here? You can't do that."

"Yes, I can. I'm going to get this guy . . . You

know, old Ted wasn't bad for a commie, nigger-loving Catholic."

Moses just nodded.

"Probably some more of these assholes around, so stay sharp."

"Don't leave me. This isn't any of my business. You said you'd let me out before we got here."

"Take your hand off my arm. Good. Now I'm going."

"You said you'd let me out."

"You're out, aren't you? Listen here, stay sharp, or you'll end up dead, and anytime you feel like throwing the gun away and giving up, just take a peek in here at old Ted. Got me?"

Moses didn't say anything, and Larry didn't give him time. Quiet as an Indian, Larry disappeared into the woods behind them.

TWENTY

Brian pulled the pistol he had taken off Jim Trawler's body out of his belt.

"What are you going to do?" Loony said. They were still leaning against the cabin. They had seen the patrol car and heard the shots. Now the patrol car was sitting still, its lights shining. And well behind the car, they had seen a shape cross the road at a slouch, disappear into the woods on Stone's side.

"I'm going to do whatever needs doing. You stay

close to the cabin. They try to come out of there, use your knife. I'll be back quick as I can."

It had been Brian's voice speaking, and Loony, crazy as he was himself, was beginning to find it all a bit disconcerting.

"Where's Clyde?" he asked.

"Right here," came Clyde's voice, and as Loony watched, Brian's face twisted, molded, began to look like Clyde's. It was wild. Like when impressionists on TV imitated someone and managed in many ways to look like them. Brian had Clyde's voice and mannerisms down pat. Could it be that he was really possessed? Loony decided he'd find that hard to believe even if he were on glue—which he wished he were. His hands were starting to shake and the reality of life was fanning away the fog of his dreams.

"Stay," the Clyde voice said to Loony. Then, turning, Brian/Clyde moved into the woods and was gone. Loony thought one more time: How in hell does he do that with his voice?

The water on the stove had started to boil and Becky turned the burners to simmer. Then, picking up the axe, she went to Monty's side.

"Boiling?" he asked.

"Yes," she whispered. "His voice, Monty . . . that's him, the kid who raped me."

"It isn't him. He's dead and buried."

"I know that voice."

"It's the kid doing it, mocking him."

"It's more than that."

"The dead do not return, that's all there is to it."

"The skeptic is back."

"Seeing the future is one thing, but possession, which is what you're suggesting, is another. The dead are dead. The kid is imitating the voice. I suppose it is possession of a kind, possession by a memory. The total acceptance of a deranged mind. But there is nothing uncanny or supernatural about it. We all have the ability for that sort of mimicry, and our subconscious is far more alert and complex than the surface, or conscious mind. It can pick up all the fine details of a voice, even the words in a language, and teach the conscious mind to speak it.

"This kid is as mad as a hatter, that's all. You've got to realize that. If we're going to beat him, we have to know we're not up against something supernatural."

"The psychoanalyst returns."

"This hardly seems the time for us to get into an argument."

"Monty, I'm telling you, that's Clyde's voice. And you can give me all the psychological mumbo jumbo you want to, and I won't be convinced."

"Okay then, you're not convinced."

"Do you remember what he said, about how he wanted to be first . . . with me? I told you that from my dream, remember?"

"I haven't doubted your dreams, really, since that . . . that image I saw on TV."

"Everything I saw is coming true. There's nothing—"

"The girl on the porch, you thought that was you. If you can be wrong about that . . . We could pull out of this. It's possible. Aren't you the one that's always belittling me for giving up easily, for being weak? Aren't you the liberated woman, or is that just bullshit talk?"

"Maybe it is," she finally said. "Maybe everything is just so much bullshit."

* * *

Loony, without glue fumes in his head, with his nerves pricking his skin like thorns, lost his cool and disobeyed Brian/Clyde's orders. He needed something to burn energy. He wanted to cut someone. Maybe get a little off that woman.

He looked up the drive, didn't see anyone.

He should wait, he knew that. If he didn't, Brian (Clyde?) would be angry.

. . . He moved his knife from hand to hand. Thought: To hell with Brian, he's nutty as a pig in a tow sack.

Moving around the edge of the house, he ran by the open lake window screaming, "Trick or treat!"

Monty and Becky saw his masked form race by, saw him stick his tongue out at them through the slit in the mask.

Larry was inching up next to the woods on the other side.

Stone, who still thought Larry was behind the patrol car, had glanced neither left nor right, and the mask he was wearing did little for his peripherial vision.

Larry, who had been raised by a father who knew the woods and knew how to hunt, crept slowly toward Stone's position without so much as snapping a twig.

"The goblins," Monty said. "The mask. It all makes sense."

But before Becky could respond, they heard a tinkling of glass. A knife blade slid between the sill and the paneling of one of the windows on the driveway side. The blade moved briskly up and down, from side to side, prying the paneling loose.

Monty laid the gig on the floor. He took the axe

from Becky. Trembling, moving quietly, he crossed
the room and swung the flat end of the axe against
the knife blade.

He hit the blade solidly, but the knife did not
break. Instead, the paneling sagged, struck the
floor on the left-hand side. Through the opening,
Monty could see the kid, his masked face pressed
against one of the unbroken panes. The kid gig-
gled, started to jerk away.

Monty made a wild swing with the axe, hurled it
through the glass. It shattered the window and hit
Loony in the forehead, bounced away. Loony made
a short barking sound, stumbled backward two
steps, wavered a moment, clutched the crown of
the mask with a shaky hand and ripped it off.

A huge saucer of blood widened on Loony's
forehead. He made another two steps backward
and fell flat on his back. The knife dropped from
his hand and he lay still.

"Gotcha!" Monty screamed.

Then he heard a shotgun roar.

Larry crept up slowly, cautiously, until he pin-
pointed Stone in the sniper position. After a moment he took in that the kid was wearing a
Halloween mask. That made him think with a
smile: *trick or treat?* He lifted the riot gun. The
weapon was loaded with alternating slugs and
double-ought buckshot; Highway Patrol theory being the slug took out the window and the double-
ought took out the man.

No windshield here. Just a kid in a tree with a
mask on.

It was a bit of a distance for the riot gun, but with
the slug as the first load, Larry felt confident.

He eased the trigger, shot Stone through the neck. The slug tumbled at such velocity it snapped the neck bone in two and nearly tore Stone's head off. The Halloween mask went sailing, and the blast launched Stone from the tree and carried him for a Peter Pan dive into the pine needles. His legs thrashed and his left heel beat an unrhythmic tattoo against the ground before body functions ceased and he lay completely still.

Larry was contemplating the surprising fact that the sniper had been white when he heard a sound behind him.

He turned, lifting the riot gun. As he raised it, his eyes took in the bore of a revolver which seemed as big as the mouth of a subway tunnel. The tunnel belched. And a train went into his mouth, took his lips and gums with it as it made its exit out the back of his neck.

As he fell, his right hand dropped and his finger reflexively jerked the riot gun trigger, causing him to shoot off his own kneecap. It went rolling out down his pants leg like a runaway tire.

The worst part about it, Larry thought, is I'm not dead yet.

Brian remedied that. He bent over the cop, put the barrel to Larry's right eye and made pudding of it when he pulled the trigger on the .357.

That finished, Brian crept toward the patrol car.

Nothing happened.

No one moved and no one took a shot at him.

He looked inside the car. A cop lay against the dash. His head had been turned to grease and gristle.

Brian bent, looked beneath the car. There were no ankles or squatting knees to shoot at.

Creeping to the front of the patrol car, he eyeballed around the edge of the hood. No one was there. That was all for the law.

He began to trot down the lengthy drive toward the cabin. He didn't bother with Stone. He had seen the patrolman fire and he had seen Stone's neck go to pieces. Even a snake dies without a head.

Moses had eased back into the pines and made love to the shadows. From his hiding place, he heard Larry fire the riot gun, and from the same position, he saw Brian come out of the woods on his side and cross over to the other. Then he heard a pistol shot, the shotgun again, followed by another pistol shot. Then he saw the kid again, creeping around the patrol car, and finally back toward the cabin.

He could have killed the kid when he first saw him, he had time, but he was deathly afraid he might miss, and he had a family, and some lost hunting dogs (Christ, he'd just left them running about loose) to worry about. If he had missed, the kid might not have. Then where would he be? Under some goddamn pine tree with his brains blown out, that's where.

Besides, he was scared. So scared, he had shit his pants.

When he heard the shotgun, Monty looked out the window and saw only the car lights. He ducked down, pulled the paneling back into place, and pushed the nails into their loose holes. It wasn't much, but it obscured outside vision, made them less of a target.

He wondered about the shooting that followed the first shotgun blast, but didn't come up with any concrete ideas. Only one nebulous thought circled about in his head—the kids had reinforcements and were shooting wildly, blowing off steam before they blew off heads.

He looked down at his hands. They were shaking.

If Monty had looked again, he would have seen Brian, running toward the house with the pistol, bounding like some sort of demon in the moonlight, the grotesque Halloween mask with the rubber knife in the skull flopping and wriggling like an absurd antenna.

His hands were shaking, but Monty felt for the first time in his life as if he had balls. His father was wrong. He did have balls. He felt like letting out with some primeval war whoop at the thought of having done in the kid with the axe. It had been ugly and brutal, but he felt good about it and could not make himself feel any other way. He wished good old Billy Sylvester was here today. He'd make him eat a dog turd and smile while he ate it.

He glanced at Becky. She had the gig cocked open and was holding it before her like a lance. For some ungodly reason passion pumped through him and he had an erection. It was the killing and the potential for violence that was doing it, causing him to become feverish with a strange kind of lust.

Lost in his victory, Monty abruptly realized where he crouched. With the paneled window in front of him, his back was exposed to the unpaneled window behind him. Pimples of ice freckled the back of his neck, made the hair there go prickly.

He looked behind him.

No face was staring through the shattered window.

He duckwalked over to Becky. "You all right?" he said, rising to touch her.

"Did you kill him?"

"Dead as he can get."

"Good," she said softly. "How many more, you think?"

"No way of knowing."

"I love you," she said.

"I love you too."

"No matter what, I do. Remember that."

"Never doubted it."

Brian found Loony's body and he was very angry. Real angry. He told the giggling sonofabitch to stay put, so what had he done? Just the opposite.

He kicked Loony in the ribs, and in an overwhelming flash of anger, lifted the pistol and shot Loony's corpse in the face—twice.

Or rather Clyde did.

Brian said, "Easy, Clyde, easy, man."

Clyde said, panting, "I'm all right, all right. Just get that teacher cunt, let me have her. I want her heart."

"I will. We will."

"*You've been saying that, goddamnit!*"

"Now's the time."

"Get the knife. Use the knife. I want it done with the knife. Cut her. Give her to the God of the Razor—rape her with his dick—the knife."

Brian patted the scabbard knife in his waistband. "Right here, Clyde."

"*Now!*" Clyde said.

Inside, Monty and Becky heard voices. Two

distinctly different voices. The crazy kid was at it again, talking for two. Maybe. Monty found that he was beginning to wonder.

Monty moved to the kitchen, found a butcher knife. He could hear the voices outside. First one, then the other.

Observing Becky out of the corner of his eye, he saw that each time the Clyde voice spoke, she tensed. He knew she was having a graphic instant replay of the rape in her head, and it made him crazy with anger and hate to realize it. He did nothing to control either emotion. He fertilized them, let them grow and blossom.

The voices stopped.

Monty and Becky held their breaths. For a brief moment the world seemed to swing back to normal. The cold night air eased through the broken window and smelled of the lake and the pines. They could hear the lake lapping at the shore, and somewhere, far away, a nightbird calling.

Then came a sound at the front door, like something heavy falling. Monty had a feeling he knew what the sound was. The girl's body being pulled down.

But why?

The answer came immediately with a whacking sound.

The kid had picked up the axe Monty had tossed at Loony, and he was playing Paul Bunyan with it on the door. He had moved the body so there would be room to swing it.

The axe struck with a loud, hollow ring that turned into a squeak as it was withdrawn.

Again and again. *Bam! Squeak! Bam! Squeak!*

Clyde called with each blow, "Trick or treat, assholes. Trick or treat!"

The axe rang one last note, flashed silver through a rent in the doorway, squeaked, and was gone.

Silence.

Becky gripped Monty's arm, and Monty gripped the butcher knife until his hand cramped. Without speaking, he moved away from her, across the room toward the door. He stopped by the boarded window, listened.

Still nothing.

He waited for the axe to start up again, realizing that it wouldn't take much more before the door went. Strips of it had fallen away, and Monty could see the night and the glow of the patrol car's lights through the rips.

But the axe did not start up again.

Then Monty had a horrid suspicion, and even as he was turning, what was left of the glass in the window across the way blew, and the kid came leaping in (slivers of glass clinging to his clothes, the axe gripped in both hands), and the force of the leap struck Monty and knocked him back, jarred the knife from his grasp and sent it sliding away into shadows.

TWENTY-ONE

Monty and Brian rolled across the floor, Monty struggling against the axe with both hands.

Brian worked the weapon loose and slammed a short chop at Monty, but Monty jerked his head to the side, and instead of his face splitting wide open, it took off half his left ear.

Monty gripped the axe with one hand, pushed his other into Brian's face. His fingers slid up under the mask and knocked it off.

Brian twisted his head away from Monty's fingers just as Becky stepped out of the shadows, the frog gig cocked and raised.

And Clyde's voice screamed, "I'll ram that goddamned thing all the way up your ass, bitch."

The voice struck her like a blow, and she remembered it coming out of another face; remembered Clyde in her, his sex exploring her innards like an alien tentacle; the explosion of his seed inside her, the grunts of his savage pleasure as he finished.

She threw the gig with all her might.

Brian ducked.

The gig scraped along his scalp, peeled a strip of hair and flesh away, clattered to the floor.

At the same time, Monty hit Brian in the face with his free hand. It was a bad punch thrown from a bad angle, but combined with a twist of his body, he was able to roll out from under Brian and scramble away on his hands and knees.

Brian tumbled to the floor, came up, went for Becky with the axe. He swung it and Becky jumped back. The axe came down on her foot, splitting through her shoe and into the flesh between her big toe and the next.

With a screech, Becky jerked her foot out of the shoe, and before Brian could swing again, Monty was up and rushing him.

Brian heard him and turned. Monty grabbed the axe close to the head and tugged.

Brian kicked Monty in the crotch and let go of the axe.

Monty stumbled backward.

Brian pulled the revolver from the waistband of his pants and fired twice.

The slugs struck Monty in the hip, knocked him against the wall. He slid to the floor.

Becky leaped on Brian's back, her fingers clawing at his face.

He spun, trying to throw her off, but she clung tight, bent close and buried her teeth in his neck, tasting his blood. And it was sweet—sweet as revenge.

And around and around they whirled, Brian trying to shake Becky, and she clinging to him with teeth and nails, legs locked around his waist.

Brian ran backward, slammed her into the edge of the bar. But she still clung.

He rammed backward again, and this time Becky felt a shock that ran the length of her spine. Her teeth came loose from his neck, her legs weakened, and when he bounced her against the bar a third time, she tumbled over it and onto the floor.

Brian leaned over the bar, bringing his feet off

the floor. He smiled, pointed the revolver at her and pulled the trigger. It clicked on an empty cylinder.

Becky rolled to her feet, dashed for the stove and the pans of boiling water.

Brian tossed the revolver aside, came after her, drawing the knife from its scabbard.

Grabbing one of the pots, Becky whipped it around and splashed the boiling water into his face. The pot handle burned her hand so fiercely it tore flesh from her palm when she let it go.

Brian howled, dropped the knife and grabbed his face.

Becky ran at him, hit him in the chest with both palms, rushed past him.

Brian stumbled, went down on one knee.

Becky grabbed the gig from the floor, cocked it and turned.

Brian was up now, holding the knife. There were golf-ball-sized patches of puss on the right side of his face, and his right eye looked as white as a marshmallow; she had scalded it to blindness.

For a moment they stood frozen, then Brian gave it up, bolted for the window, put one foot outside and was pulling the other over when Becky jammed the gig beneath his buttocks, into his scrotum and pulled the trigger.

The sound of his scream echoed across the lake, and he fell violently out of the window, pulling the gig from her grasp.

Cautiously, Becky inched forward, looked over the sill. Brian lay on his stomach. He had twisted around so that his side was against the wall beneath the window. A pool of blood was fanning out from beneath him. His knife lay a yard away, shining in the moonlight.

I did it, she thought. I did it!

Exhaustion overcame her, and she leaned forward, weakly resting her hands on the windowsill.

And in one quick motion, Brian twisted and grabbed her, clenched her hand so hard a bone snapped in it.

Becky yelled and tried to pull free, but couldn't. Brian clung to her with one hand, and with the other he held the sill. He began to pull himself up, the ruined face coming into view.

Becky saw a long fragment of broken glass sticking out of what remained of the frame. She used her free hand to grab it, pull it out. Blood squirted from her palm, but she clenched her teeth against the pain and drove the glass into the back of Brian's clutching hand.

Brian let go with a jerk, taking the glass with him.

Becky stepped back from the window just as Brian made it to his feet. He held his hand in front of him, looking at the glass sticking out of it. He didn't pull it out. He dropped his hands by his side and looked at her.

But he did not come for her. He staggered back, turned, started walking away, the gig dragging between his legs.

He fell to his knees suddenly and stayed propped there for a moment. Then he fell to his stomach and began to crawl.

Brian said, "I hurt . . . Hurt something awful." He began to crawl in a tight circle, like a dog that had been fed broken glass.

Clyde's voice: "You dumbfuckingasshole . . . you stupidsonofabitch."

". . . for you, Clyde . . . tried for you . . ."

"You did one peachy job . . . the cunt gets away. Hear me! Gets away."

". . . sorry . . . so sor—God, it hurts, hurts something awful . . . so bad . . ."

"You're going to ride the blade . . . ride it, you sonofabitch . . ."

". . . I know . . . I know . . . but you'll be there . . . where I can see you. Clyde, answer me . . . answer . . . me."

". . . Yeah . . ."

". . . you'll be there . . . to see me?"

"I'll be there . . . we both get the blade now, you . . . sonofabitch . . ."

"I . . . I was never a Superman . . . like you, Clyde."

". . . tell me what I don't know . . ."

". . . I . . . I love you . . . Clyde."

". . . you too . . . you dumbfuckingsonofa . . ."

Brian lay still now, curled in a fetal ball, the gig poking out from between his legs obscenely.

Becky rested her injured hands on the window-sill, leaned way out, yelled, hoping he would live just long enough to hear:

"Trick or treat, you motherfucker?"

TWENTY-TWO

Becky went over to Monty, crying. She knelt by him. He did not turn his head to look at her.

"Monty?" she asked softly.

He did not answer, just looked straight ahead. She pushed the hair off his forehead. "Monty?"

"I'm here," he said softly.

She bent, touched her lips to his. "Bad? Are you real bad?"

"Right arm is broken. Think I did it when I got slammed against the wall. Think one of the bullets kind of bounced around inside me, went down into my leg. I don't feel so good from the waist down. Can't feel much."

"Oh, Monty."

"Don't worry, baby. I'm not going to die. I hurt so good, so goddamned good. Like maybe I've seen heaven on the other side . . . and you know what, Beck?"

"No, Monty, what?"

"God carries the biggest damn club you've ever seen."

It made no sense to her, and she didn't try to fathom it. "Monty, I'm going to make you comfortable and go for help . . . Hear me, baby?"

But her voice was lost on Monty. He had made himself a dream. And in this dream was Billy

Sylvester, and he had Billy Sylvester down, and he had his knee on the little shit's chest, and he had a candy wrapper with the biggest, greasiest, nastiest, stinkingest dog turd this side of a garbage-eating Saint Bernard's ass, and he was forcing it down Sylvester's throat, and he and his little brother, Jack, were laughing like lunatics, laughing so hard their voices bounced off the face of the moon . . .

After she made him comfortable, she walked out of there in search of help. But a patrol car met her before she had gone too far. They put her in back with a man who smelled of shitty pants, and he said he had been around when the shooting started, and he had run to a cabin five miles away and called some law.

Becky leaned back in the seat and wondered how it would be now for Monty and her. She felt oddly certain there would be no more images and black dreams living in her head. But how would they see the world now? They had been over on the dark side and tasted a moment without rules and logic; and once those rules had been broken, shattered like wine crystal, she wondered if those pieces could ever be gathered and properly glued again.

She could only hope, and the ability to do that, to hope, meant everything to her.

EPILOGUE

After Monty and Becky had been driven away and the bodies had been hauled off, a small devil duster kicked up where Brian had lain, twisted, gained velocity. It whipped around the cabin and howled like a mad little boy, rattled the glass in the windows, then it moved toward the lake where it finally played out over the water, leaving only a ripple to show its passing. And the ripple only lasted a moment, then the lake was dark and quiet and still.